Things to Be Survived

Tales of Resolution and Resurrection

Scott Tinley

HabitusBooks

A division of TransPac Publishing Group
San Diego • San Francisco • Santa Barbara

For information, please contact:
Habitus Books
P.O. Box 221, Del Mar, CA 92014-0221
HabitusBooks.com
or the author directly at ScottTinley.com

First printing 2006

Printed in Korea

Headline Printing & Graphics, Cardiff, CA

ISBN 1-4276-0794-X

Library of Congress Control Number: 2006938296

Some of these stories were previously published in the literary journals *War, Literature and the Arts; Fiction International; CityWorks Press; Tattoo Highway* and *Dream People.*

Also by Scott Tinley:

Racing the Sunset

Finding the Wheel's Hub

Triathlon: A Personal History

Sports Endurance (with Ken McAlpine)

Although this collection includes both fiction and non-fiction prose, it is not always obvious which is real and which is imagined. It is the author's express desire to let the reader make that distinction if they feel they must, that it places the text somewhere where they can come at it comfortably. And while just a few of the characters are real with real names, the rest are based on the experiences of the author. He makes no claim to their existence and any imagined connection to living persons are left to the full responsibility of the reader.

To all the raw and rummaging scribes who pick up a pen because they just don't give a damn.

Special thanks to my family and friends for putting up with my cynicism, Mac Williamson for cover work design, Harold Jaffe for guidance and every person who has ever pulled themselves out of life's ditches.

Table of Contents

Preface

Thoreau went to the woods because he, "wished to live deliberately." I wrote about survivorship because I was tired of living in deliberation. I wanted to make some sense of all the death, all the tragedy I had been exposed to. It was the blood shed by my family, my friends and bodies I'd never see again, even though I'd never known some of these bodies as living people. I didn't own the tragedy, but somehow it had invested itself in me. And as is often the case with language and thought, I had to create enough fiction to actually get close to its truth.

These stories and tales have become close friends, many having been written and re-written over a five- to six-year period. The words evolved as my memory and imagination played hopscotch with each other. Some fictions became dangerously close to actual occurrences and some of the non-fictives ran off on their own, afraid of their shadowy realism. To use the ancient Italian cliché: *Se non 'e vero, 'e ben travato.*

"It may not be true but it is well-conceived."

There were times when I felt sentenced by some unspoken conspiracy to solitary confinement. *I used to be happy* I called from my literary cell. Parts of me were being urged to tell no tales on the grounds that many had it worse than I and we were all susceptible to certain methods of explanation. And even if I could finally write truth in fiction, there would be virtually no one in my circle of influence who would care to hear about it.

I thought often of the Italian writer and political theorist, Antonio Gramsci, who was imprisoned under Mussolini's fascist regime for nearly 20 years between 1926 and 1945. Gramsci, widely considered one of the greatest minds of the 20th century, penned nearly 3000 pages of critical and cultural theory while indentured in a tiny cell outside Turi. I came to know his "pessimist of the mind, optimist of will" doctrine as if we were old neighbors, speaking over the back fence. I found solace in those who'd subverted their suffering and teased out the most fertile interpellations, morphing the demons into allies of the spirit. There is responsibility in survivorship.

The time to hit "print" was clear.

There are a number of recurring themes inside these stories: struggle, uncertainty, irony, quest and not accidentally—ambiguous war, which is to say, any war. But what I was striving for was salvation in the most unlikely of places—in the rents and seams, the margins of our sometimes banal existence where meaning and purpose hide and get co-opted by popular culture; where the content runs roughshod over the context and something profound happens in the soft underbelly where survivorship is born. I don't know if I found it, but I am more settled for having penned it. My edges seem less frayed. For this, and the fact that I am able to pay it forward, I am grateful.

I didn't write with any shame or perversion. Honesty never corrupted anyone who didn't deserve the favor. Rather, I went after the indifference of people who would rather not examine unless voyeuristically as they slowed on the freeway, searching for body parts on the opposite side of the road. In the end, that darkness needed a stiff wind to blow the screaming yellow tarps away.

What every person looks for in their life is their own salvation and the salvation of the people around him. I realize the re-presentation but can't write it any better: It begins with the discovery of exactly who you are, and if you're lucky, the discovery (or at least the hint) of what your purpose might be. It then continues with the fulfillment of your own innate, Creator-given powers, the love of others and the love of life itself. I do not believe it is possible to find this in yourself, by yourself. Not alone. My characters in the book discovered this, as did I.

We humans are a social breed. Even Defoe's real-life Robin Hood, Alexander Selkirk, found that after his four-year and four-month indenture on Mas a Tierra in the Juan Fernandez Islands, he was unable to re-adjust to a home and family. Upon his rescue and return to England, as much as he wanted to be with others, to revel in the company he'd so missed and then had trained himself not to, his ability to embrace his own existential bliss had been thwarted by the years of a solitary life. Isolation had mutated the pecking order of his happiness and he died of fever while sailing off the coast of Africa.

Sometimes a man will rebel against himself. This rebellion is part of testing how far he will go in his suffering to find that true self. If he is to find that purpose without trouble, then he would find no meaning to his existence. It does seem that true existentialism—the study of our existence—has always been a perfect meritocracy.

As I re-worked these pieces over the years, I found a sense of joy in existential purity, a kind of John Belushi Zeitgeist without the tyranny of thick fame and exigency of thin ego. And the culture of fear so pervasive in our society began to lose its grip on me. If I had ever felt that I was devolving into a mere dot in a dot.com world I would remind myself that it wasn't so much as finding myself but loosening the false shackles of someone else's making. I merited existence by denying that I wasn't anyone other than who I was. The stories don't so much reflect as reveal. Some things the characters beat. Others they join.

In this collection, characters suffer for both the right and wrong reasons. If I made things happen on paper it seems that I wouldn't necessarily have to go through them again. And those around me I cared about might also gain this hall pass.

Maybe the evolving mise-en-scène may just have been my memory shaking hands with my imagination. Or it could be a final acceptance of my beautiful neuroses. It matters little.

There is such reward in pathos because it reminds us all that we are humans regardless. My characters taught me the pleasure in allowing some sadness in our life, of embracing the pain, letting it inform us and then pass right through. And after awhile, a funny thing happens—we are able to see ourselves in all the craziness that surrounds us, all that wonderfully edible mayhem, living and breathing, dying and laughing, not in the shadows but in every sunrise and every sunset, howling at the high noon moon. The whole process is very orgiastic and may help explain how the human species has survived when others have become extinct.

Survivors get to suck the marrow, to know that as they die they will not discover that they had not lived.

S.T.

Imagined

Eros, Poseidon and Me

"Darkness, darkness, be my pillow..."
Jesse Colin Young, singer, song writer

There was no one to call to file the edge off. Or to sharpen it that it might open a bottle or book. My dog knew—animals are smarter than men. Buddy swaggered unhurriedly across the room, looked at me with been-there-it-hurts-like-a-motherfucker-don't-it? eyes. He didn't lick me or curl up at my feet. Maybe he knew that I had to fall through the hole in myself. Dogs don't waste your time with empty sympathy. The pain left only two options. And I knew she would be pissed if the blood stained the new beige 4-ply carpet.

How hard can it be to snatch something real from the ever-fleeting, to do a thing for the thing's sake, to see the rottenness in life but ignore the smell and reach for the broom? How fortunate was I now, as I had been in the past, to have my own Betty Ford Center two blocks away?

I put an old 3/2 mm wetsuit in my backpack, tossed some wax, the rest of some half-hearted bottle and a mushy apple in the front basket. I grabbed the first board out of the rack and tucked it under my arm.

I don't remember coasting down the hill on my bike or scrambling down the bluff as the sun left its mark on the hellish day. I couldn't tell you if it was a beautiful sunset or a cloudy dusk. I knew that it was getting dark all the way around; the sea and the sky welding at the horizon.

Buddy stood on the shore and pointed like a bird dog. Strange for a mutt. "Go home. Go home! Ah, well then forget it, suit yourself." I took a bite of the apple and tossed the core into the sand watching grains stick to it like memory to the soft part of the brain. An after-hours gull snatched the lucky find.

I thought I knew her. I was sure. In the end, it was like the others, shadows of potential, possibility smothered by daily silence. Was it me or them?

Paddling out I began to notice things I hadn't before: the way the cold water seeps in around your knees before your waist, the way the little wake comes off the tip of your board in angular v's, going somewhere, no where. I noticed how the shallow spots on the reef created circular boils on the fast-dropping tide, pulling water, energy and life from its center back into some black hole beneath the surface, a place from which that life and water were born.

There was only one other guy out, one other surfer in the lightest part of the dark hoping maybe, for one last toothy wave of a two-hour session. He only needed a ride in, didn't have to worry about being caught from behind.

I paddled right by him, avoiding his stare. Nothing he could say would've made a difference. Maybe he was just out of the joint and hadn't surfed for three years. Maybe he was a "trustafarian" who surfed every day to avoid the boredom of excess. I turned my head just enough to lift my chin.

"Word," I said.

"Word up," he replied.

He paddled away. I didn't see him leave the water or walk up the path, only heard a dog bark.

Out of the corner a big set started to well up on the outside reef. How far had this wave traveled only to finally release its energy here in six feet of black, kelpie salt water? Some orgiastic physics would never explain it. I paddled hard, spun at the last minute and dropped in, one with the falling lip, Rosetta stone in sync. At the bottom, I laid it over hard and felt the board bite deep into the wave's face. Anger and regret driving me.

I could've done better with her.

The wave in front now, feeling the rocky bottom, standing up, begging to be held like a child bringing home a picture made at school.

"Look, Dad. Look at this picture I made for you!"

Look, son, look at this wave I made for you.

Inside now, an absence of feeling in my heart, there's darkness at the wave's circular core. It's a place of hope and I strain toward a feint pulsing glow, the glimmer of some left over refracted light off the bluff as I squirt out onto a broad, nurturing shoulder understanding in some small way what Frankl realized after surviving Auschwitz, "What is to give light must endure burning."

Where does wisdom and perseverance like that come from? Can it be applied to relationships?

Paddling back out, I glanced over at a sea lion. He returned my stare with a queer look, as if to say, "I can do that." The ocean could swallow him up and get nothing. He made an obscenely joyous bark. It was a tempting sound.

The sky above me reflected only blackness. I surfed by feel, wondering what it would be like to feel the shark's first strike. Pondering what it would be like to die in such novel way, eviscerated by what tomorrow's paper would call, "A killing machine that came out from beneath the ocean's surface to rip the man's leg off." The autopsy might find that, "he had, left ventricular hypertrophy, an enlarged heart, possibly due endurance training."

It would be a fitting death; all that heart muscle just blowing the red stuff out.

The moon was now the only witness. I sat for a long time and watched the lunar reflection creep over the edge. It was a teasing light, teased by flowing clouds. And sometime after midnight that great block of ice that had settled in my chest began to melt. I wanted to believe that shit about truth at first light but I felt that it was the night, the absence of external fire, the melding of one day into the next that opens the gates. The rain started; loud but soft on the back of my neck.

In the beginning she was real. Now she changed her eye color with tinted glass. Was I creating my truth or rehearsing my death? Was she?

Almost imperceptible at first, I begin to notice it first in the waves I choose and the way I surf them. Then in my relationship with the ocean surface, the way my board sits gently upon this sheet of smooth black ice, the way my hands softly make quiet little circles on its skin.

I cannot see the advancing swell but I sense something gathering up, waiting for me. I paddle hard for the horizon, the lower stars blocked by this advancing lump. Harder now, pulling at still water, onward to meet her. I am a guest, open to invitation and experience. She is the women, the mother, the wife.

When she finally comes, it is like no wave I have ever ridden: big but not unwieldy, imperfect in shape and texture, uneven and raw. She carries me gently but I cannot stand, content to lie prostrate, my face close to hers.

Following the shelf, I ride until my fins hit the sandy shore and I stay there, motionless, breathing. The moon bends under a passing cloud. A phosphorescent edge of foam is switched on.

I let the match burn all the way through before grabbing my board and walking toward the cliff. My footsteps kick sand into the air.

She is gone now. They are gone. Buddy is there.

I see her older shadow moving in the dark, digging in bent trash cans outside the theater looking for someone new to play her part. We are making choices in the moment; choices that matter, that hurt.

She still carries that edible mayhem in her, dying and living not in the sunrise but in every south wind. I thank her for the madness and the adventure before saying goodbye to her gentle violence and half-dead eyes.

I've met someone else, I say to myself, tasting the words. *She comes and goes. We are…old friends.*

Walking back up the wet clay trail, Buddy waits for me at the top, laughing, I imagine, at how humans confuse absolution and the absolute. I know that surfing and what is left of my life are there now glaring back in the headlights of a passing train.

I am not haunted by her.

Over Her, Over Me

"War cures all neurosis."
Anna Freud

The call came in at 3:35 A.M. It's always around that time when the real fuck-ups come out. Why don't they disturb other people's lives during normal business hours? The P.D. routed the call after they'd sent a unit out on a noise disturbance complaint. When the officers arrived on the scene and poked around the apartment, they smelled smoke and called us.

Sometimes the lazy cops or the rookies or the guys who got their ass kicked in poker last week will call the fire department prematurely. Still, most of the calls like this are a tease, like a friend's wife who likes to flirt. We live for the ones that come in as a "fully involved, working fire," the sound of urgency straining through the consistent calm of dispatch. Dragging a charged two-inch hose into a Douglas fir and stucco-fueled hell, licking that bitch with a sweeping fog pattern, laughing at the top of your lungs; that's no job, that's a drug.

On this night though, we wouldn't get that jolt of watching flames spill through the roof and lick the sky like some giant tongue in search of its prey. No, this one was different. It might hold a place in our memories alongside the best working fires of our careers, but that place would be well sealed and unavailable to all but the ones who had to go there from time to time. God's chisel would not change that night.

It works like this.

The call comes in over the "George Orwell," our name for the loud speaker, and wakes all of our asses up. There are twelve of us in this station: four on the pump, four on the ladder truck, two desk jockeys, the Captain and a Battalion Chief who wishes he was still pulling hose instead of pushing paper.

Two of us double as fire fighter/paramedics and respond to medical calls and structure fires in a box ambulance we call "the rig." I've never called it an ambulance. I suppose it's just a superstitious thing and all; like the way fighter pilots avoid using the word "crash."

I was on the rig that night and something in the air or on the ground or in between left me less than my Teflon self; the emotional landscape I'm used to where nothing sticks. Maybe it was the burritos that firefighter Carter made for dinner, the argument I had with my wife before coming on shift or the two strings I'd broken on my guitar earlier that evening. Probably it was nothing at all. But I didn't expect happy dreams.

We lay in bed, hoping for a quiet night unless it's something worth getting up for; something real…that drug.

But we're jerked awake by "the George," recalled from wherever our minds had taken our bodies. Some of us pray a bit, if the early day has not been kind and we are so inclined, and then listen for the dispatcher to tell us which unlucky bastards have to climb out of a warm bed and go deal with the side of life God didn't spend enough time working on.

We don't all pray to the same God, but the presence of danger has a way of bringing you fully alive, frighteningly aware of things like the way dogs circle around their bed before lying down or the way a house always smells better when kids and fresh bread and cut wood is around. The presence of fear, even thimble amounts, will make you wonder how we all got here in the first place, trees and dogs included. When you're on shift, you look at life in full color, full time. There are no black and white images. You pay attention to everything, and you pray, hoping that your prayers don't just go out the window behind the smoke of somebody's cigarette.

And on this night, this December 10th, the year nineteen hundred eighty, miserable *can't make up its mind* weather outside, not raining, not dry, more like the clouds were dripping a cold sweat, the George Orwell sent the pumper on account of the smoke.

I whispered a little "thank you," not really caring to who it was directed, snickered at the thought of Captain and Larry and Cala and Carter having to put on cold, clammy turn-outs, probably still wet from that practice hose lay we did before dinner, and go chase some hokey, "smell-of- smoke," bullshit call. I know that Carter is hoping the cops will get in the building, find nothing more than burnt spaghetti noodles left on the stove and turn them around. But it ain't going to happen. My stomach does something and I lie there, listening to the rain and the men.

Nobody complains about it in front of Captain either. He cuts us a lot of slack and it seems he has always known what we know now. We save the wimpy complaints for each other while washing the trucks or drinking beer after work. Some of the guys will dump on a new girlfriend who might listen for a spell but the wives, well, they mostly have had a guts-full and tell us that if we don't like it, we can quit it. But that isn't likely, knowing in our hearts their ain't a better job when you pull someone's ass out of trouble or get dealt a quiet shift and just work around the station, relaxing after five with a Scrabble game or a few songs out on the porch; just watching the rest of the nine-to-fivers head home to their wives and their kids and their homes.

Sometimes I wish I was one of them, knowing that when they went to sleep, chances were slim to none some old man would be calling them up to come and put him back in bed because his legs were all stoved up.

But when I am getting off of work in the morning, nothing planned for the day, a full night's sleep behind me, and I see that same guy headed to his office to drive a desk all day, well, I'm not in too big a hurry to switch lives.

The clock on the wall says 3:36 A.M., four more hours until I can be home, a bit later if I stop at Moonshiner's for some eggs and a game of pool if I see a truck or two I know out in the dirt lot.

Dammit all, though. No sooner than my head falls back into the pillow, dispatch comes on again and says for Medevac 12 to respond with the pump. "Possible woman down," I catch, while scribbling down the address in case we get split up from the fire truck.

It's my turn to drive this shift and my partner, Tommy Willard, a fresh, young kid right out of the academy who's only working his second go-around, is still wrestling with his helmet in the corner as I fire up the rig and chase the pump out the big bay door into the moonless night.

"C'mon Probie," I goad him, "You ain't gonna' need that skid lid with me at the wheel." Tommy jumps in, slams the door just before it gets ripped off the rig by the station wall and tells me he only wears it "on account of he don't want to be seen with a guy as ugly as me." The kid still on probation has balls. I like him a lot.

We drive through the dark, empty night, silent in our thoughts, the occasional siren used only to keep night owls honest. There's a pissy rain keeping even the hard core drunks holed up in some place of their own making. I am awake now, alive and watching the strobe lights of the big pumper truck in front of us reflect off the dampened avenues. The city's asphalt street-veins are deserted except for a couple of red trucks and a half dozen grown men who got lucky enough or stupid enough to find them living out the fantasy of many young boys. I get a strong sense of ownership at times like this; like the well being of this little town sort of belongs to me and the crew. I know any one of us could mess up bad in a heartbeat. But the responsibility doesn't scare me and we are as fitting to the job as bark to a tree. We share meals and stories and lies and truths.

I look over at Tommy as he's picking up the mike to go 10-97 (arrived on scene), a look of thinly veiled anticipation in his eyes and I wonder if he will have the same feeling when he is as old as me, has seen what I have seen, and has dealt with the ambiguity behind it all. Soon enough he'll realize that human trauma is greedy. It deserves all of our attention.

3:42 A.M.

We park the rig beside the pump, grab the med bag, 02 bottles, de-fib machine and haul ass up the stairs just behind Captain, Larry and Cala. Carter is the engineer so he stays with the pump panel. He's okay with that. He has a couple of kids now.

The probie trips on the first step and I don't even think about laughing. Until we do our job and clear the scene, nothing's funny, not on the inside nor the outside. We aren't hired to play God, but we ain't selling stocks and bonds either. I used to feel things. Now I don't feel much at all. And I'm better at my job because of that fact, just keeping my empathy wrapped up cellophane tight, an old sandwich setting in the back of the fridge. Maybe you'll get around to eating it before it goes bad on you.

P.D. has finally gotten the locked door pried open and we all enter the mysterious apartment and source of the loud music and smoke. We go in as a tribe more than a group, a collection of cogs in a machine, one that has the ability to alter some natural law of living and dying. But the only thing I know for sure is that I won't stand for people going and getting hurt or suffering needlessly on *my* shift, even if I don't feel much of anything about it later.

Captain has a strange sense of forecast—he's seen it all many times before in his duty with this city. He's the kind of man who will leave a mark on the world, unlike most of the ones you meet who just get marked up.

Something's not right, his eyes and gestures tell me.

Waving the others back, he motions for me to come along, confident in our time and years. Not much gets through the veneer that this job has given me cause to grow. He turns slow as a dime store Indian and asks directly, "You're a Beatles fan, aren't you?"

3:48 A.M., 3:50 tops. I put the thought of the juevos rancheros at Shiner's out of my mind and focus my light on Captain's big yellow-coated back as I follow him down the long smoky hall. "NFD" it says, Nashville Fire Department. Or NO Fucking Dying. He's not really human at times like this, but part predator and part angel. If he ever got killed, I think I might go ahead and pray to him too.

We reach the closed bedroom door and can clearly hear a John Lennon song through the walls, "*instant karma's gonna' come and get you...*" But what almost knocks me off my feet is the smoky scent that initiated this run. It is not the familiar smell of burning wood or plastic or clothes or even the unmistakable stench of crispy bodies. It is the sickly sweet stench of too many cheap candles. I've seen it before, felt it, and wondered about it at hippie weddings, weirdo funerals and Catholic Churches where you get a year of credit in Purgatory for each cheap little blue candle that you pay to light.

Cap nudges the door open far enough for us to get a glimpse of what it is that will leave another fucked up imprint on our minds; not if, but a question of degree. I had called the candles right. There must have been dozens of them all lit up in shapes and sizes, pyramids, globes, long skinny cylinders, headstone masts from a hundred sunken ships illuminating a no man's land between this life and the one after. Heck, there over on the chest of drawers next to the stereo was a candle shaped like Mickey Mouse, a glowing red, yellow and blue flame between his wax ears. Full color, full time.

At the foot of the bed was a shitty 13-inch TV, the

screen showing the snow pattern that used to come after the 11:00 News was over and before cable brought you people trying to sell worthless crap that you wouldn't buy from a neighbor at his garage sale just to be nice. On one wall hung a suggestive, stylistic poster of a man and women, framed together like two pieces of puzzle, he on top, she on the bottom, naked on the bed. It was photographed in black and white but I could have made it color by blinking my eyes.

And there, lying wonderfully serene in the middle of her bed, was a majestic young lady dressed in bell bottom Levi's and a lavender flannel pajama top. Her long blond hair straight, thick and shiny in front, matted wet and red, molded to the pillow in the back. She seemed like she would have been easy to love. And though I fought the emotion, I hated her for that.

It was then, as the old cassette player switched to "In My Life" and I heard the words "with lovers and friends I still can recall", that I looked around the room and realized that we were in some type of Lennon shrine.

I stood over her, her eyes still wide as in search for some meaning to it all. But I still had to verify the condition, document the diagnosis and get "permission" from the hospital not to work her up. When someone opts to eat a single .44 caliber bullet for dinner, there just isn't a lot you can do for them.

I got the hospital on the radio, trying not to look as the Captain took off his glove and closed her eyes with his rough, weathered hand. Larry, a regular hose man from southern Nebraska and the best bass fisherman among us, walked down the hallway after having scoped out the rest of the apartment. He was humming Dylan's "Lay Lady Lay" and when he peered into the bedroom and saw the Cap with his big mitts on the girl's face he spoke the line, "his clothes are dirty but his hands are clean." The words left his mouth without malice, nor thought, nor intent. Stuff like that comes out. It just does. You don't even think about it at the time.

I hung up the phone and Cap pulled the sheet over her face. I tried not to but still, I told him what he already knew, but that I needed to say, "There's no excuse, no damn rhyme or reason. It's as simple as that. Bitch had to go and die on our shift."

Like I said, some private transaction with the ordinary unlucky, on a regular shift.

And as I turned away to leave the room, the edge of my coat knocked over a candle, dousing a single flame and spilling hot wax onto my grimy, black rubber boots. Oddly, grotesquely, secretly, I admired her courage, disdained her cowardice, wished I could have known her in another life and felt the heat from the warm wax.

Captain came over and looked at me, his eyes asking if I was all right.

"Life's an accident but death ain't," he said and went outside to have a cigarette.

I just nodded, ignoring the coroner's arrival and asked Tommy to drive the rig while I sat in the cab on the way back to the station. Watching the sun trying to rise and break through the passing front, dancing reds and yellows peering through the grays, I told myself that this must be the way with firefighters: process the emotion and move on. You don't think about a young child's love for his pet puppy when you are dragging his little body out of a burning building. Caring will make you soft, I told myself. Yep. Thinking will ruin you.

I asked Tommy if he believed in God.

"On the good days," he told me. Not an unexpected reply.

"You?" he asked, pulling into the station driveway.

"Oh yeah," I whispered, "Because it's amazing how much blood can come out of one little body."

We walked back inside just as the morning news

was coming on. Well past 6:00 A.M. now. A hair-sprayed talking head was reporting on last night's murder of John Lennon outside his Manhattan apartment building. The young crew was crowded around the TV set, making referenced jokes about the call last night. Just another defense mechanism, I thought. Let it go. How could they have known what John Lennon meant to his fans, to the world, to the girl last night?

Tommy, who was 4 years old when the Beatles first came to JFK Airport, was coming up with the best lines, building his own protective layer, one cynical crack at a time. Yep, that's the way with firefighters— risk it, defy it, Betty's Crocker or Dante's fucking hell. Do everything humanly possible to drown Darwinism with 5,000 gallons per minute from a charged hose or 1000cc of Ringer's Lactate direct I.V. Later on, diffuse it all with laughter; just give it away.

God, Allah, the Great Spirit, fucking Santa Claus…we aren't any of these guys. Hell, we aren't even docs. Not on this night. Not ever. We're just firemen, veterans of a different kind of war.

I sat in front of my locker and took off my turn-outs, trying not to look at the melted wax on my boot. Tommy walked in and asked me if I wanted to get some breakfast when we got off shift in a few minutes. My eyes, filling with tears now, looked up at Tommy and gave him his answer. He stared at the floor, not quite confused, not quite embarrassed and tried to say something. But no sound came from his mouth.

I drug my sleeve across my face, got up and headed out to my truck. Passing the Battalion Chief in his office, it was 7:30 A.M., twenty-four hours since I started this shift. Nothing's different, I lied, just a day in the life, another collision of empathy and emptiness.

"Don't forget to do your Patient Run Report before you leave. Number's got to be right."

Sure Chief, I thought, numbers have to be right.

Sometimes patients, sometimes victims.
Always numbers.
Always human.

The sun was fully operational now, the bright colors reflecting off the panes of my truck's windshield as if the glass itself were on fire. Reaching first for the bottle of Jack Daniels under the seat and then for my old Martin acoustic behind the cab, I swallowed hard and wondered if I could still play it. Tears were streaming down my cheeks, salty raindrops onto a spruce body, I was exposed in the morning's light, a cracked shell lying on the wet tarmac, the truth exploding out of my gut like a running dog unleashed.

I sat on the truck's tailgate, a street fight happening inside my heart and watched as my fingers went right for the rosewood neck, hitting the frets slowly but accurately: D, F#mi, Em7, A and then A7, just like the first day I taught myself the song several lifetimes ago. I mouthed the words to myself, "*Pools of sorrow, waves of joy are drifting through my open mind...*," took a long pull on the bottle, setting it down next to the guitar, knowing they deserved each other.

When I looked up, Captain was lumbering out to his own truck, a big duffel bag full of firefighter stuff slung over one shoulder, just enough teeth showing in his smile to let me know that he knew and that he cared as much as he was able.

Cap set the bag down next to my rusted tailgate and sat down on it. He was carrying a bag like we all do: dirty t-shirts, a couple of magazines on fishing, hunting or cars, a Tupperware bowl that held cookies from yesterday morning, a few tapes, maybe a Bible, maybe this month's centerfold. Everything smelled of smoke. Mostly the Bibles. A lot of important things aren't easily cleaned.

I passed him the bottle but he shook his head and

grunted, reaching instead for the guitar, inspecting it like he was considering a delicate piece of art. Then he played one strange chord way up on the neck, reached up to the gold tuners and gave the low E a gentle twist, altering the sound in a way few could tell.

"Flatten the low E string just a tad. Gives that song a raw sound and fills out the bottom some."

And then he got up to leave, passing back my axe as he would a newborn.

Walking away, he stopped, turned just slightly, enough so I could hear him but not see his face and said in a voice softer than I remembered him owning, "Not much left to kill or die for; nope, not too much left at all."

"Well," I chocked back a reply, "If there is I reckon we'll see it first."

"Yep, I imagine we well," he said. "See ya tomorrow, huh," not asking but confirming, and threw his duffel bag in the back of his truck.

Everything else could stay here at the station.

Sailing . . .

Sam Jenks walked up the gangway to the marina's security office. Something was shifting inside her, deeply, like a baby carried in the later stages of pregnancy moves as it tries to get comfortable, like tectonic plates during an earthquake. Sam carried the weight of her thoughts and what had just happened as roofers carry tar and heavy paper up ladders for homes that they will never live in. The smell and the asphalt under their finger nails won't wash off until they quit the job. Or it quits them.

Samantha L. Jenks wished she was a quitter.

She could see that the door to security was open and stopped before it. Sam turned slowly to look around the marina at all the boats, the same as she'd done many times before. But instead of reading the names of the boats and wondering about their origins, Samantha watched a lone sloop move out past the jetty, a single figure raising the mainsail from the cockpit, surrendering, she thought, a white flag to all that lay beyond the man-made rock wall.

She could change places with the figure but was chained to the past, shackled to last night. Or was it the night before...

She finished the vodka martini in one swallow and it helped a thought slide into her head. There was no direct connection or relevance, she mused, just a dreamy bar-note. Something that snuck in under the radar.

There was that song jumping out of the speakers set in the low ceiling— *And I was thinking to myself, this could be Heaven or this could be Hell.*

Sam didn't know because she didn't care. Another thought entered her mind.

Why did they always name boats after women? Women's names, painted in dark-colored script on the transom. Just the way that men had the balls to put a women's name on a boat's ass, like they were pinning their own rite of ownership on some woman's tail because, they would say, she'd made them *feel* something in their salty, shallow pasts.

"Well, feel this," she spoke into the empty glass like a microphone, unembarrassed but glad for the attention that brought the bartender that brought another Absolute and something. But she was thinking too hard now, the self-loathing finding its way up through the rented confidence and the smoky air of the Harbor Bar and Grill; definitely more bar than grill.

Her mind went back to some undergraduate class in sociology. They had discussed Gramsci's theories of hegemony, of the patriarchal society still controlling the elements, large and small. Salary discrepancies, educational opportunities...boat names. She had the *pessimist of the mind* part down but the *optimist of the will* seemed to have gotten stuck back in her dorm room when growing up was more of a concept than statement of fact. She was one of them now; the result of an imprisoning re-definition of language. The verb, *growing*, had become the noun, *grown*. And she wanted to throw it up, her doctored-hair falling all around the porcelain, the vortex of age spinning down. But always, the tank refills itself in mockery.

She ordered another (*so I called up the Captain, please bring me my wine*), said to make it a double and when the bartender's eyes darted toward her and the ends of his mouth spiked upward, she straightened her back, stood up straight as she was taught in school, unhinged herself from the stool that seemed to sprout from the long mahogany bar with people's initials carved into it.

"Is there a problem?" Her tone dancing on a thin edge between sarcasm and challenge. "Would you like to see my I.D. *again*?" She was playing with him now. But he was too young to see it and a little empathy crept back in, waving its finger at her like a parish priest. The bartender's face screwed up tight and his young skin tried to wrinkle around the eyes and mouth but hadn't learned that trick yet.

"Hey," he asked the women whose age outnumbered him by ten, "Who really needs a fifth martini?"

She read his name badge—*Dylan*. "The person who just finished her fourth."

He pushed the drink in front of the women and managed a sardonic, "whatever, lady," smile.

Whatever, buddy boy, she thought, and then half-apologized to the place he had just stood. But he'd be just like all the rest, if she let him, slick as tanning oil. And within a month, maybe two, escaped over the fence, pieces of her heart left like bread crumb hints in his wake. Grand theft soul—there ought to be a law against it. And she'd go on sleeping with yesterday.

That's when the voice lofted over her shoulder, nicking it on its way down. He ordered two beers—Guinness, for Christ's sake. That was like drinking liquid bread, motor oil. Un-American, she mused. But booze knew no boundaries.

He sat down at the stool next to her and moved it *away* from her, almost into the lap of another man.

One more martini and she would've asked him if he thought she smelled bad. Instead she made little animals out of her napkin and looked at her watch every 94 seconds.

"The past doesn't pass away so quickly in here, does it?"

"Excuse me?" She had heard the words, even knew what he meant, but still wanted the luxury of digesting them before replying.

"Would be a shame if..." he tried to continue but

Sam cut him off.

"If you're looking for the neuvo-hippy philosophy student, I'd suggest *The Dreamscape*, over by the campus. But they don't serve foreign beer."

"Have you ever been inside that place?" He turned full and faced Sam, regarding her with a curiosity that seemed to have its own volume control. She reached for her drink and twisted it to the right, clockwise, safely.

"Not since I was a graduate student. And I felt old then." She noticed that he was plain to look at; painfully ordinary clothes, a Timex watch, no belt, Levis that weren't even pre-faded. But his hair fell across one eye and he made no move to uncover it. He wore no after shave to her thinking.

"They have one wall completely covered in old chewing gum; the saliva from a thousand coed mouths stuck layer upon layer. It's..."

"It sounds hideous," she interrupted him again but then wished she hadn't but plowed ahead. "Imagine what it's going to be like to clean."

"Oh, that won't happen," he was sipping from the separate mugs in no particular order. "The owner of the building is a friend of mine. He put it right in the lease that the wall will never be scrapped or painted."

She looked for the pale white teeth to show or his head to nod in anticipation of the obvious joke. But they never came.

"You're serious?" Her tone more accusation than question.

"Of course. And the rent goes down each year as the wall grows with gum and the square footage shrinks." This time he smiled. A little.

There was a long silence and she returned to her napkin, now recognizable as a giraffe shape.

"Camp tricks?" he motioned to her creation.

"No. I ran away with the circus when I was twelve. Hanky the Clown took me under his wing, taught me a trade, helped shape my life out of napkins dripping mustard from corn dogs and teriyaki beef-on-a-stick." Her creativity surprised her.

She set the giraffe in front of him to examine, waiting for the forced laugh that always came with the forced conversation of the lonely. But it didn't come and the man simply put two chips where the ears might be. "A girelephant, my favorite animal."

"Camp tricks?" she asked, slightly intrigued.

"Naw, saw a young girl do it at the Wichita circus while standing in line for the spin art display."

"She looked like you, only older."

"Yeah, sure. Listen to the lyrics—*we are all just prisoners here of our own device*."

His name was Kive Fender.

"Like the bumper?" she asked.

"No, like the guitar. Hippy parents and all." He put out his hand and said nice to meet you.

"But we haven't yet."

"Haven't what?"

"You know, met." She threw her head back and laughed her first honest, nearly infectious laugh all night. Her name was Sam, not Samantha, and they shook vigorously, like German businessmen.

"Promise me one thing," Sam's eyes narrowed and the laugh that had brought a little tear ran her mascara like rain on charcoal. "If we get to the point of banal conversation, and I'm talking Sears and Roebuck stuff, you'll stand up and leave without drama or phone numbers or empty promises."

Kive said he couldn't promise that because he'd always done his shopping at small hardware stores. Banality was a foreign concept, not so much rooted in arrogance but intuition.

"I'm not good at lurking," he said, "around people that I can't grow old with," and paused to take a sip from the second Guiness, "within a couple of weeks."

Sam scrunched up her nose and thought he was different. But then they always were at first.

"I'm hoping for functional disenchantment," she tried to sound coy but some truth to her testimony had leaked out. "Either that or remain in this current state of constant escape."

"You must've had some bad ones," Kive rubbed his brown eyes.

"Oh, you don't want to know, honey. The history of my relationships has situated itself," and Sam took out her gum and stuck it on the long, damp bar, spreading it out with her left thumb, "right here."

"Promise yourself something," he asked, "you know, request for a request." But Sam said only maybe, she was either too smart or not smart enough to make trust a fixture in her future.

"If you ever get to that sad wisdom of compromise," Kive continued unphased, "you'll look in the mirror instead of across the room."

"You sound like my brother," Sam moved the subject to a different truth and looked across the room for the waitress. "He's a commercial fisherman with a Ph.D."

Kive seemed to like that image.

Kive Fender had a boat in one of the slips that was attached to the rock jetty that supported the restaurant that was more bar than grill. He'd just moved here from Spokane and would spend weekends on the boat, just messing around, as he put it, *because he could*.

"Does she have a name?" Sam asked, not sure if she meant the boat or any female liaisons.

"Not really," Kive removed the chocolate-brown hooded sweatshirt that had made him look like a monk. He didn't expand his answer.

Sam stood up to leave, thinking they had skipped to the point of banality, had landed at the central tendency much quicker than usual.

"I thought I was supposed to do that—you know—leave first so that you don't have to."

"Are you trying to be chivalrous or something? Because you'll mutate the pecking order if you do." Sam brushed the chips from her pants and tried to remember who she was supposed to meet at the bar in the first place.

Kive stood as well and looked at the chips on the floor, cracked pieces of wasted time. "Was it a string of bad ones or just one whopper?" he asked. "Because you're wound is defining you."

Sam looked around the room, it was filled with tourists and yachties and people who were all too happy to be lonely in the company of others. "Who are you?" she asked, wanting to know. "Did you just watch *Brave Heart* or something?"

"No," he told her, "I think it's more like *Jeremiah Johnson* when he builds the log house for the Indian women and the mute kid; not so much chivalry or duty, just regular necessity with accidental goodness."

They walked out together and when Kive noticed how deftly she steered herself from one handrail to another, he knew she was well-practiced in self-pity, good at hiding pain. Or at least pickling it extra-dry.

"Wanna see my boat?" he asked.

"Do you know how many times in the past few months I've heard that line?" She tried to sound matter-of-fact.

"Yeah, I can imagine."

"Can you though? Can a guy really know what it's like to hear the same shit over and over? Knowing full and well the code, having cracked it at eighteen but still speaking it like you'd been sentenced to state your wedding vows in pig Latin?" Sam's anxiety was leaking down her cheek.

He helped her down the gangway as he would a

grandmother or a child w/crutches, speaking as they moved. Sam allowed him to. And that surprised her.

"No, no he can't. But I think it's important to try and create linguistic guidelines that rise above the biological, don't you?"

The fresh air had a sobering effect on Sam and she reigned in her heart from the sleeve that it was perched on.

"I'm not that advanced in the sciences," Sam was protecting herself with glib again. "And I don't know much about Italian cooking."

"I see," Kive smiled and Sam asked him how much he could stand of her cynicism. "Oh, a lot," and then added, "If I'm learning from it."

"What are you, Mr. Bumper Guitar? A shrink or a Zen Buddhist?"

"Naw, just a cop. Well, here it is—my unnamed vessel."

It was as plain as Kive: almost thirty feet long, single mast, a non-descript sloop, sails furled under a dark-brown cover, simple, clean. And no name. Sam walked to the edge of the dock and checked the transom to make sure.

"Loretta's Rendezvous", she mumbled just loud enough for him to hear in her flat didactic tone. "Tina's Escapade, or the more thoughtful twists: Sea Me-Feel Me, Abby's Absolution and my favorite—Mermaid Dream." The boat names had bubbled to the surface like some wicked Disney character, carrying with them the emotional film of oil and diesel.

"Men in a constant state of escape, playing with grown up toys and women's lives by using them as faux icons, the bodies left on shore, the image taken to sea." Sam was in her stream of conscious rant, subjected to the trickle of memory. She grabbed a mast shroud and stepped over the cowling without asking and sat down in the cold fiberglass cockpit.

Kive, still leaning against the piling on the dock said, "Do you think *Hotel California* would be too much of a cliché? Hey, go ahead, make yourself at home. Welcome aboard, I guess." He watched the girl from the bar fiddle with the coiled main sheet, wrapping and unwrapping it around her wrists like she'd done it before. There was something ageless in her eyes: part child, part guilt. Kive had seen it once before when he was a kid. It was in his mother after the letter from State Department had come informing her that her young husband had died gallantly, "defending his country," the letter inside the plastic-windowed envelope had said. It took him sixteen years to realize that she didn't hate him for going. Kive's mother had tried to retreat into her youth, circling the wagons around her kids and then pretending she was one of them. But the sadness had betrayed her. The change was huge and black and permanent. Widowed, they'd say, like the spider. The softness stayed around the red under-belly but the outside was case-hardened.

The long silence on Kive's boat was not altogether uncomfortable. There was the wind to listen to; always the wind with its ability to make soft dreams or nightmares out of its sound.

"Wanna go out?" Sam asked, looking up at the man on the dock who seemed happy enough doing nothing.

"Are you asking me out on a date?" Kive cocked his head to one side but Sam was the better actor and read the body language.

"No, you stupid *man*," she had coiled the end of the main sheet into a hangman's noose with thirteen coils. "I'm asking you if you'd be interested in taking me sailing on your nameless sailboat."

"Oh, I see." Kive was putting his mother's memory back in the box. "And I'm assuming that you want to go now, like before tomorrow when you're sober and less in touch with the far side of yourself and can write me off as what? Capital?"

Sam listened for the harsh tone but didn't hear it.

She wanted to hear the intentional sting so she could go back to the safety of the bar. But something was shifting inside her again, and it scared the hell out of her. She pulled herself up, held her long hair behind her head and leaned over the back of the boat. There was a coughing sound, like a person preparing to start a speech. And then she vomited quick and hard with a degree of urgency as if it felt good to rid the body of something that shouldn't be in there. Kive stepped on the boat and placed his hand lightly on Sam's shoulder.

"Don't touch," she spun around, bits of a turkey sandwich dangled from the corner of her mouth and the early tears that'd bled her mascara became dark vertical rivers.

"Okay," Kive said and opened the gangway hatch with a key from his pocket. "But I'll have to see if I have a matching costume down here when we go to the *Kiss* concert." He handed her up a towel, only his arm visible from the galley.

Sam turned her head, took the towel and watched his hand, wide and clean and rough hewn. She thought it looked like the last scene from *Deliverance* and started to laugh, queerly as first and then harder, like water running downhill, picking up steam in the tributaries. Kive came up holding a glass of something amber-colored and Sam was doubled over in laughter, small bubbles of spittle and food and horror forming around the corners of her mouth. It was an infectious sound, an essential purge and he half expected to look over the side and see little devil fetus' floating to the surface.

He dipped the corner of the towel in the bright fluid, drank from the cup and dabbed the edges of Sam's mouth like a dental hygienist. He leaned closer to Sam, whose laughter had morphed into an intermittent gasp for air, and looked at the transom.

"Where the Dreamscape has gum, I have your lunch. Think I'll leave it there. Could be the beginning of something."

"I'm a responsible person, you know," Sam willed her tears away. "I can care for most things other than myself. I have a Chia pet now, working my way up to a goldfish."

"You are unique," was what she remembered him saying before she passed out, "and a darkly intriguing mystery."

She didn't remember him carrying her to the forward berth or the soft kiss on the forehead or the way he watched her breath come and go until he knew she was safe and went up on deck to watch the stars do the same.

In the morning it took Sam a full minute, seven minutes in dog years, to remember where she was and how it'd all came about. The man, what was his name? Something from the 60's or Hawaiian sounding. Different. No, not that different. But maybe. He'd been cutting to the quick of her, the blade shiny and bright.

Sam had woken up on strange boats before. Boats always felt kind of...noir at night. But there was something encouraging about them as well. Not so much in the sailing but in the way they rested peacefully in their slips, tied to the dock, safe behind the long rock jetty in the lee of the high bluff. She envied them. They had a different sort of appeal in the morning than at night. But they hadn't moved, looked the same. Everything around might've changed but the boats woke up to their same fiberglass and aluminum and wooden selves.

Not so with Sam. She knew a *morning after*, regardless of the environment. Everything was different in the morning. And everything was the same. The later was what kept her down.

He was gone. Or at least not sleeping next to her in the small forward v-berth. Too many times they were gone. Too many times they stayed until it was too late. Or she did. There was that stock analyst with the big power boat.

Flat screen TV, DVD, two wet bars, two gold chains and a tan line where his wedding ring would be. He'd asked her if she minded leaving after they were done.

"What? Like I should just walk over to my own half million dollar yacht at four in the morning? I don't even remember where my car is. And I doubt it will start without pushing it." He'd called the night patrolman, Jackie, a friend of Sam's who took her to the office and made up the cot for her. It wasn't the first time.

Her life seemed to be stuck in a bad film loop with the projectionist on break. That's when she saw him. The body of Kive Fender was slumped over the chart table, a yellow legal pad serving as pillow. That's hard to sleep that way, Sam thought, and saw his arms dangling below like fleshy afterthoughts. She'd seen dead people, lots of them back when she was an ICU nurse, when she was alive herself.

Sam knew that this man was dead.

It was that old story but it's always kind of new and dark and not entirely unwelcome when it comes. But it gets olds quickly, like fresh fish. Each moment holds its own power and resonance and becomes part of your historical landscape, not later but at the exact moment that it unfolds. The real treason of time isn't that it waits for no one but that we alter its effects as filtered through memory.

Sam had removed this filter, cut it away with a rusty saw when her own child had died; just never woke up. Not even a year old. SIDS, she knew all about it, had written a paper on it in a Pediatric Disease course in nursing school. After that she had burnt the landscape behind her, lost the father or maybe chased him away. She knew it but still had buried the reality of her actions along with the child and the resulting fire that ash-coated every moment before.

And now, the haze of the same salty smoky bar, the string of escape-artist men and something about the boats had become its own filter. But in the truth of morning Sam would tell them they were a distraction, thank you very much, you've quieted the embers. Now I can go play hidden vampire for another sunny day and wait until happy hour.

Sam pulled the thick woolen blanket back, was surprised to see that she was fully clothed, socks and all, and moved over to the man's body. No pulse, skin cold, not even clammy, rigor mortis already setting in. No sign of trauma, it had to be a massive MI, a myocardial infarction. God dammit, Sam cursed, trying to call up some fight or flight response. She wanted to feel something with the aid of natural chemicals.

I might've saved this one. He was young. They always stood a better chance.

She brushed the fallen hair out of his eyes and saw the long silver chain that had fallen out from under his shirt. It held a Chinese symbol, not a gold cross or dog tags or the man's initials. On the table next to his left ear was his wallet. She opened it and saw the badge. Jesus, Sam thought, he really was a cop. And his name really was Kive Fender.

The filter and the alcohol gone, the image of the baby returned, resting quietly in his pale blue crib, Samantha L. Jenks felt all of it.

That other morning, almost ten years ago now, Baby Jensen was sleeping later than usual.

I best go check on him. Well, maybe, I'll just have a quick shower before he wakes. A little peace before the challenges of raising a young vivacious child learning to crawl and working at the hospital with patients who are not young and dream of being able to walk down the hall unattended. Just a little peace. Just a quick shower.

Sam, set the wallet down, let Kive Fender's hair fall across his eyes as he'd briefly known him and walked up on the deck. It was warm and she looked at her wrist to where she used to wear a watch, thinking that what happened in the past was not and would never be shouldered by her alone. Only by her aloneness.

Best go tell Jackie, she thought. It's going to be a warm day.

Sam wished she had a big straw hat to live under, wished that a Trojan Horse with baby-soft Chia hair hadn't snuck into her mind, wished a lot of things. But mostly she wished for five o'clock.

Semper Free

His wife sang, "Amazing Grace" at the funeral. She just stood up there and belted it out in her forest green dress like a game show contestant, only slower, measured, with the presence of some rolling grief bunkered deep within. Little emotion scaled the walls that are built early in military life; mostly unnamed and unmentioned. They say it's protection against tragedy, that duty to a steely restraint is what's required, what comes with the job.

A few miles away at the beach, the tide was going out.

It struck me as odd, this stiff display of sound and tribute. The only black she wore was wide, rounded-brim hats that, with her full cheeks, made her look like a model of Jupiter. At the end of her song she said we're all in this...alone. A feeling of heaviness drew me to her. I didn't catch her Christian name. Military wives can lose that part of their identity.

Hundreds of perfectly-soldiered bodies stood at attention, Marines, Semper Fi and all that. They stood attentive and erect in the August mid day sun. Black dress-uniforms with wide white belts and polished pewter buckles, they were a powerful, elegant and respectful clothes. Not a single man or woman was daring to sweat. One drop of perspiration would show disrespect for the dead man—a fallen Marine, part soldier, part human. Sergeant Major Roderick T. Larimore was being laid to rest.

Scattered among the family and fellow Marines were a handful of surfers in floral prints and logo'd t-shirts. Boards were strapped to roofs of rusty station wagons and VW buses parked haphazardly behind anonymous green sedans with government plates and no hubcaps. Sun-bleached hair, loose but clean, came right up next to crisp, full dress caps. A Marine's glossy shoes nearly stepped on a bare foot.

"Excuse me, Sir."

"No worries, bro."

The Marines eyed us closely, our bare legs checkered beside their razor pleats, but not in the way you might think.

Reagan was President then. And many of the men around me were younger, just kids really, willing to go off and die if they had to, unable to walk into a 7-11, buy a six pack, a straight forty or a lotto ticket if they wanted to.

I stood in line to sign the guest book behind our older friend, Uncle Billy. Nobody at the beach we called home knew exactly where Billy was from or if he really had any nieces or nephews. Billy had always just *been*. We watched the enlisted men print their name and rank neatly on each line, salute the corporal attending the table and move stiffly to the left. Uncle Billy, on the north side of forty in his face, half that from the neck down, took the pen and bent over the table. The attending corporal watched oddly as this aging surf bum pulled his long gray-blond pony tail back behind his head and drew a perfect tiny wave in the guest book. In thick block letters he wrote the words, "*Operation Starlight, Batangan Peninsula, Sept. '65,*" across the face.

And then Billy signed it, "Capt. William Johnson, 101st Airborne," raised his right hand in something resembling a salute, but his fingers closed one at a time, like he was counting into a fist, and he stepped to the right. The officer stared straight ahead before turning slightly to his left and spoke quietly to Uncle Billy. It seemed an unfamiliar tone for a Marine.

"Used to draw those on my pee-chee folders back at Bakersfield High. Had a nice one on the front of my helmet at Quang Nhai."

I told Uncle Billy I didn't know he was over *there*. He said sometimes he didn't know either.

"You get any medals or anything?" I regretted asking as soon as the words passed my teeth.

"Naw. Not like your grandfather in *his* war."

I went quiet, just like I always did when people brought up my family's past, their wars, their medals, my family of soldiers. My dad the drunk.

I wondered if Billy was digging things up or re-burying them and thought that his time of peace-making must've come and gone. Some day I might talk to Billy about Vietnam. But I'd wait until he talked to me about it first. I might've earned the conversation because of my family's past. The most truthful thing I knew about the Vietnam War was that it wasn't a war as much as a context, a way of unexplaining the explainable. Age had nothing to do with it. My dad had been and took his only son with him in ways neither of us could unexplain.

I never knew Marine Larimore; saw him just once. It was down on the beach near a surf spot we called Devil's Slides. A wide sandy cove, usually safe enough on the inside, but farther out on the point the waves broke hard and fast over a shallow, rock shelf that Billy told us had probably been created by a rockslide from the cliffs that rose from the south side of the cove. It was a weekend, a Sunday I recall. More families and wannabees than the locals cared for, but made tolerable by an oil can or two of Foster's. The Slides' cove hadn't been the same since they'd built the concrete stairs down the cliff. Nothing ever is after the cement hardens.

The morning had been big and thick on the low tide, vertical take offs, heroic tubes, a few broken boards. Small crowds in the water that way, but just a hint of fear below our cool veneer. It was the kind of swell that you talked about for weeks, but not for months or years. Those only came in the winter when the sandy cove was nothing but lonely rock and dying kelp. Johnny had been out, Strider, Will, me. Not Uncle Billy though. He rarely came down on the weekends, said he didn't like to be a part of, "the whole Village People thing."

Later that afternoon we sat on the beach in the high sun, rubbing our toes in the warm sand, calling each other pussies for not going for it. Most of the crew was still there. It was better than going back to the beach cocoons most of us rented. We worked at night, if at all. Billy was the only one with any steady work, or at least with a regular skill. He made custom sails for the rich kid's small racing sailboats, had his garage converted into a miniature loft. Sometimes we'd go over there during the day when there was no swell and just hang out and watch him work and listen to the old jazz records he had playing and think how oddly comfortable he looked working that heavy duty sewing machine like a skilled grandmother whipping out a new dress for a little girl.

As the sun moved slowly in the high summer sky, Larimore's boy walked up to the group of us. How he chose me, I'll never know. He looked twelve, thirteen tops, had his hair cut high and tight, green shirt, white lifeguard zinc on his nose.

"Excuse me, sir. Can I borrow your surfing board? I'd like to try it."

I was tired from the morning's session, probably a little buzzed too. Maybe the twang of guilt that crept into my conscience from time to time was poking around. Whatever, he'd caught me off guard. Johnny started to say something but I shot him a look I'd learned from my old man when he was trying to dry out and I'd gotten in his way.

An old thought of my dad swept through me and caused chicken skin on my arms and neck. It was when I was ten, half my life ago and he was home on leave from his last war, for the government anyway. Mom had given up on him around the time he'd chosen to do another tour. At that age, I didn't know what was worse—a new school every two years or a dad who chased an extra few stripes on his arm by letting Uncle Sam have more say in his life than his wife and kid. He wasn't around much. I made the best of it.

"Yeah sure," I told the Larimore boy. "Try not to bust it, kid." I wasn't going to say *be careful* though. Let him paddle around the shallow inside. I couldn't tell if I was trusting his imagination or my hopeful projection. The wind changed directions and freshened. My mouth tasted of metal and I spit in the sand.

The kid picked up my board and walked back to his mom, dragging the fin in the dry sand. She was a tall woman, not heavy but thicker than what I remember my mother looking like before she finally left him. Her hair was a deep black and pulled up under a straw hat with a little chin strap hanging loosely on her neck. She was bent over two sandy-bottomed girls near the water's edge like she was picking fruit or working a rice paddy. One of the girls was holding a red plastic bucket and a yellow shovel, the other was building a sand castle. It was a tight structure, detailed with crisp angles.

The mother stood up above them, proud, pregnant, and looked at her son dragging my board toward her and then intently over in my direction. Her hand moved toward the sky in a kind of wave. But it seemed more in recognition than thankfulness.

"Hey kid." He turned and asked me, *yes sir*, again. "Be careful. It ain't Miami Beach out there."

"Yes, Sir."

"Hey kid, what's your name anyway?"

"Junior, Sir. Roderick Junior."

The war in Southeast Asia had been officially over for eight years but the hurt and the pain and duplicity of it all was still fresh. Everybody wanted to forget, so we buried the idea. Only some people's role would never allow it to go farther than just below the surface. As hard as they tried to push it down, the memories would bob like a cork and with it all the shit that oozes out of the rottenness that is war. The vets I'd known, friends of my dad, could turn on a dime, seemingly at peace one moment, lost in torment the next. The smallest things would catalyze it, like a dark haired mother in a straw hat bent over a child.

The kid tried to pick up the board, knowing he shouldn't drag it, but it was awkward for him. He got it to the water's edge and slid himself up over the tail toward the nose, like he was crawling under a wire, and tried to paddle. There was a lull in the shore break and he eased himself out into the bay and fell off the side. A few of the guys laughed but I was ripped back to that time when dad was finally home for good. Even the Nam wouldn't take him anymore.

He'd asked me one Saturday morning what I felt like doing and I told him it might be fun to go over to the park and shag some fly balls. We were doing pretty well until I hit one on the roof of the concession stand. It was a nice hit and I could see that my dad was pleased, but it was our only ball and then dad tried to get up on the roof by climbing a chain link fence. He made it up with some crazy leap from the fence to the edge of the roof and seemed real proud of himself.

"Hey kid, your fuckin' old man still has it." Dad yelled in my direction.

What did he have though? That wasn't the first time I'd heard him talk like that. And the way his eyes kind of went in different directions when he stood up on the roof, took off his shirt and wiped his sweaty face with it. He threw the ball down with a conviction that scared me. Then the cops drove up.

They started in on my dad right away, yelling at him to get down, to keep his hands where they could see them, all that over-zealous cop shit you see on TV. I thought it all a big joke at first, the way dad was taking his time climbing down, ignoring their threats over the P.A. To my dad they were just a couple of young punks in cheap city uniforms.

And when he told them so, they tried to get him in some kind of cop hold. But the army and the war and something dark and unnamed had taught him, changed him, made him...*different*. Even at ten I knew it wasn't his fault. He scared me a lot.

One minute I was catching fly balls against a pale, October sky, and the next, I was looking at two cops laying on the ground, one was unconscious, sprawled next to the black and white cruiser with an imprint of a gun butt on his temple, the other was pinned to the ground by my dad's foot, his cheek ribbed with asphalt pellets and a small river of blood oozing out of the corner of his mouth. Standing over him was the man who had retrieved a little white ball off of the roof, reciting his name, rank and serial number over and over. I didn't know this man.

He started drinking again during the trial, and when he finally got out of the brig four years later, I knew him even less. Maybe I should've tried. But I was seventeen with an alcoholic father and a born-again mother who'd just up and left. I felt like a dog with two leashes being pulled in opposite directions when all I wanted was to yank off my collar and run free.

* * *

The eulogist at the funeral, some kind of mid-rank soldier whose lip seemed to tighten into the shape of a rain gutter as he poured the Corp right into the microphone, said that Sergeant Major Larimore was a warrior, with a warrior's heart. He had the need to be needed. He won't be around to lead and protect his family and his men. Or keep our American shores safe.

Yep, so the rest of us can surf, and wait tables at the Chart House two nights a week and not worry about much at all. Just live in the shadows, let somebody else go off to war if we ever had another one.

And then come home in a bag or a bottle of JD.

With Purple Hearts pinned to broken ones.

The dogs of my past wouldn't let go.

A chaplain with a comb-over that hung in his eyes under the heat stood up and said that memory's chisel cannot change what has passed by as *His Will*. Normally, Strider would've been all over this guy, busting us up with his scathing commentary. When I glanced his way, his eyes caught mine. They were death-row-inmate eyes; serious and questioning, part sorrow, part release.

I felt a long drop of sweat start at my forehead and roll down under my sunglasses, through my t-shirt, past my shorts and drop off the edge of my scabby knee into the earth.

"Damn, I could use a beer," I mumbled under my breath.

The word, "Amen" came from a soldier behind me.

* * *

"Dude. Check out the kid! Mid bay, middle zone." It was a tribe's voice, almost in unison. At first I didn't recognize this rare sincerity of a surfer's words. Young Roderick Junior was in a hard pulling rip, desperately clinging to my 6′ 4″ thruster, the airbrush of Jimi Hendrix on the nose pointed toward the heavens like a rocket as the current drew him out. There was no scream as Jimi's black afro bobbed in the current like a dashboard doll. Maybe Junior was embarrassed. Maybe he didn't want to bother his father who'd returned to his family with a steel shovel. The castle needed a moat to protect it from high tide invaders.

I heard the mother yell, "Rod!" and never saw a man move so quickly, except when my dad fell off the couch, pushed off by JD himself. Hang on son, hang on! But Roderick Larimore Sr. was not a good swimmer, his arms beating and pounding the surface into a salty frappe.

Three of us up quick, sprint-paddling the first board we could grab, eyes glued to the kid, sideways at the dad.

Johnny stopped at the father, told him to climb on his board and paddle sideways, parallel to the shore, out of the rip, away from his kid. Not a chance though, the love between father in battle with nature and common sense. He'd save his boy. He'd save a village. That was his job.

Johnny screamed at the father to hang on.

Roderick Sr. screamed for his only son.

The mother screamed for the men in her life.

Strider and I reached the kid just before the board was ripped from his grip by a big set. An aqua marine haze sent Jimi's image into the castles made of sand. Junior's arms were now high in the air like they could be on a roller coaster decent or when the *born agains* say, "Thank You Jesus" from the front row at church. Little Roderick's eyes were filled with some animated horror movie terror. But he never screamed for help, just figured it was his own fault and his own job to get himself out of the shit.

Strider grabbed the kid by the back of his baggy green t-shirt. It said ***31st Airborne*** in bold, blockish script. He coughed out a "thank you, sirs" as I spun and watched Roderick Larimore Sr. go under, separated from Johnny, who was in no shape to be saving anyone but his own butt. It was the same wave that pushed Strider and Junior into the beach. One in, one down.

I used to blame others for holding the key to some prison of my guilt. And here it was again, sliding lower and lower into some gallant watery grave while I tried to tear apart my own coffin and deny someone this dark water that was my home. I belonged here. This was all the family I had left. This sinking man, he had *earned* the right to die any way he'd like. But why now? On my beach, on a Sunday?

"Not now, Sir," I mumbled and sprint-paddled over to the sinking sergeant. But I could see both our chances slipping away, a few feet deeper with each timeless second. His semi-conscious fingers seemed to stretch out from his hands held high as if asking why, as if reaching for a life not his own to save. I dove off the board and reached for those hands, white and cold, and touched once the wrinkling tips. I could see his eyes glassing over and his lips still moving, still calling for his boy as the sea passed those lips on its way to his lungs. Down we went…together.

And I felt myself going black, my own lungs moving up into my chest and then my throat. There were stars around my eyes and I started to count them.

At three stars I saw my father's ghost.

At four, my own reflection.

And at five stars I kicked my legs and reached again for Larimore's hand.

There are points in every man's life when they must become an accountant of sorts, when they do checks and balances, cost benefit analysis, decide if the ends justify the means. I moved right past those as if they were but a metaphysical speed bump. This wasn't a numbers game; this was Darwinism, a place from whence we all come, dust to dust.

Larimore's hand was like ice, his fingers slipping and sliding out of my own and I fought the urge to panic, trying to remember how many times I had been driven much deeper than this by big wave wipeouts. If I could only get a hold of his wrist, I thought, set some purchase on our future.

But he seemed to be accelerating as he moved away from me, the distance between us moving in geometric space and time. Just before I blacked out, I turned away and swam up, a dim and dull light guiding me. When I hit the surface, I heaved salt water pain, everything in my nothingness. And my hands were empty.

At the surface, there was mayhem, people everywhere. Mostly they were screaming. Johnny paddled back out with Will, instant sobriety in their eyes. They kept asking me, "Where'd he go, man? Where'd he go?"

"I…I don't know. He's still down there. Still down…."

I puked again, grabbed a sky full of air and got

ready to go get my own damn medal. I alone knew how to find and save Sgt. Major Larimore.

Just then two lifeguards pulled up the flaccid and clammy body of Sgt. Major Roderick Larimore. They put him on a rescue board that was piloted by Uncle Billy and started CPR. Fucking Billy, he *never* came to the beach on Sundays. They were doing what they were trained for; like soldiers on the beach, doing their job.

* * *

A young girl cried and was picked up by an uncle or a brother or maybe another distant cousin. It shouldn't have been her dad. Dads don't die at the beach. Waves don't kill, only wars.

In the future, a first date's advice, a teenage fight with mom, a new man giving her away at the alter—she would repeat that phrase: It shouldn't have been my dad. Not that way. She won't remember a lot about her dad. No one takes pictures at funerals, but the images stick better than weddings and birthdays.

An acrid smell of gunpowder, I counted the guns. Twenty-fucking-one, same as I'd be in fourteen days. I had planned on a night of legally heroic drinking, planned on living forever. Peter-fucking-Pan. A horn, Taps. I'd heard it every morning growing up on the base. And came to hate it.

Two Marines pulled a large American flag off of the casket that held the body of Sgt. Major Larimore and folded it with the precision that only comes with ultimate admiration for the living. It was honor with a vengeance.

Did I dive enough times?

Actually, it's a bugle. There's one in my old man's war chest where he used to hide the bottles from mom.

Could I have gone deeper? Held my breath longer?

I tried. I really tried. Did I ever get that junior

lifesaver patch at summer camp?

One more dive, deeper, pulling that man's hand into my own, his grip on life the same.

A boy was standing in front of me, twelve, thirteen tops. A dark suit hung lifelessly on him, borrowed from a short uncle or some salesman telling his mother he'd grow into it. Little drops of tears had fallen, leaving rings of salt on the collar. They looked like ashes. He had a peely nose and held his stiff black shoes and socks in one hand, the other stuck out to shake mine.

I tried to stand tall but found myself slouching like an old mannequin whose prop had slipped in the heat of a store display window. The cool veneer that hid the war zone beneath my summer skin was cracking. I saw clearly but nothing made sense. I took his hand in mine and squeezed it hard.

A word like, "sorry" began to escape my mouth. But it was soundless air. I would've called him "sir."

The kid didn't say anything, and we looked at each other in some strange confluence of generations and cultures. I wanted to say something about lost fathers but all I could think of was lost sons. Then he glanced over my shoulder to the west and spoke.

"I'd like to learn how," the kid finally said.

I choked out a "sure, anytime," in some thinly veiled stance.

Uncle Billy came up behind. I thought he'd already left.

He was crouching on one knee, his crow's feet-framed eyes darting all around as if he was searching for something, as if they were little troughs that caught the pain and ran it off onto his cheeks so his vision would stay clear.

"You have the right to grow older, kid." Billy was kneeling so that the kid was taller than him. "And then remember all of this. But you don't have the *duty* to it. Guilt will burn a hole in man."

They loaded Sgt. Major Roderick T. Larimore into the back of a big black vehicle; a fiberglass box carried with too familiar ease into the mouth of darkness, and drove it away.

There were still a few tiny specks of sand between the toes of its contents, a few drops of salt water in its core.

I'd teach him, make the kid better than me. He'd rip.

A few miles away, the tide had shifted. Like it always did.

Centering Your Self

Wake up early. Think that it is much too early to get up.

Wake up late and curse yourself for sleeping in. Try to remember why he left you. Throw something at the wall.

And miss.

Get out of bed, relieve yourself and think back to the public restrooms you visited in Japan. Some company trip you piggy-backed with an unmarried friend, or was it a raffle prize? There was no seat in the public bathroom—you just squatted, aiming at a hole in the floor, centering your balance and urinary aim or having to face the ignominious challenge of walking around with pee on your shoe all day.

Laugh at yourself when you recall the onset of a leg cramp and having to call for that friend to come in and help you stand back up. Miss that friend. Mark your calendar, your palm pilot and your day-timer to call her. Look at your digital clock and wonder if you can still buy the kind with hands, the clock that is, not other objects inserting their way into your conscious.

Consider if time marks anything but itself. Do today's digital kids know what "clockwise" means?

Go into the kitchen to make coffee and realize that you only have whole coffee beans. Your grinder is broken. How could such a travesty be happening in your own home? Be too embarrassed or too lazy to borrow your neighbor's (you've forgotten their names anyway). Find yourself hitting the whole beans (that are now wrapped in two layers of aluminum foil) with a meat tenderizer on the cold concrete garage floor.

Wonder what the cost of a week's stay at the Betty Ford Center is.

Burn toast, scream for your kids to wake up, talk on

the phone, scribble a note on a pad and be thinking about a boy in college. He always spoke about "lifestyle." Wonder what genius named a condom after this word. Probably the same pimple-faced-millionaire-high-school-drop-out who invented the Pet Rock and the red dye number 7 air freshener for cars; Christmas scents year round courtesy of petrol-chemical evergreen.

Listen to your twelve-year-old son sing a song while he re-gels his spiked hair: "One tequila, two tequila, three tequila…floor."

Realize that multi-tasking turns one to Prozac, Xanex and Danielle Steele novels. The antidote, you think, is one tequila, two tequila.

Then four.

See your fourteen-year-old daughter's *Seventeen Magazine* on the kitchen counter. Realize you're not exactly sure of her birth date. Consider getting your hair cut like the model on the cover.

Take a call from your Aunt Tally. She's the one with the little tattoo who was arrested for something that currently slips your mind. Recall the time your mother called her a "jobless-lesbian-hippy-rock-star-wannabe."

Wonder if you'll see your mother at the reception Tally has just invited you to. Remember how Aunt Tally took you outside at family parties and taught you to play HORSE, basketball's version of strip poker; how she made you laugh when she tried all those crazy shots; promised you that you wouldn't get pregnant from playing spin the bottle, Twister or kissing with your mouth open. How she laughed at herself but never at you?

You're not recalling the times so much as you're recalling your last remembrance of them. That way, memory sort of reclaims itself and time moves out from some kind of straight line to a group of overlapping circles, like a Venn diaphragm, like a rock thrown in a pond, like answers from a Ouija Board.

Recall that Italian cats are supposed to have twelve lives. Ponder what life you are on, if any. Think that Aunt Tally must be an Italian cat.

Have a conversation with your spouse as you rush to get your kids out to meet the school bus, the regular sized one, not the short bus. You asked:

"Did you return the video?"

He said, "I saw your aunt buying rubbers at the store the other day."

"So."

"Well did she mention if she could get us tickets to the game on Saturday?"

"Here is your blood pressure medicine."

"I didn't know you needed a prescription for condoms."

"I want to go to the opening of the clinic she worked on."

"When did she go into construction? I thought she lived off of tips from playing at the coffee shop."

"You are impossible," you think out loud.

"Hey, maybe she's a switch hitter, she always had a thing for Tony Gwynn and Elva Degenerate." He laughed at his own barb.

The longer you stay married, the closer you grow apart.

Wonder why you said yes 18 years ago, choosing this life of serial monogamy.

Then remember the intimacy and smile but feel the corners of your mouth fall down like old socks. But recall the roses he bought you last week and the way he washes your car every other Saturday, the time he said you were so perfect he had to make mistakes for you. He's an imperfect man but knows when to give up the Karaoke stage.

Hate that term, "The grass isn't always greener"...blah, blah. Screw that. Stifle a single tear. Just how hard can it be to snatch the present out of the future? To get health insurance that covers the terrifying oxymoron of "marriage counseling?" To lie with your mate without the intrusion of another man's face?

Say God dammit out loud for forgetting to feed the dog this morning. Feel like you are chasing two escaped dogs running in opposite directions. Wonder who you really want God to damn.

Turn the radio on while you drive to work and go through all 12 preset buttons before you find any music. It ends quickly and you put in a Self Help tape your sister gave you while you put your make-up on in the rear view mirror. A man with a very soothing voice tells you to close your eyes. And so you do. Until you realize you're about to have a head-on crash with an SUV-driving soccer mom who is putting on her make up in the rear view mirror, one hand gripping eyeliner, the other smothering a matchbox-sized cell phone. Whatever happened to the "two and ten" grip from driver's ed?

Say, "Thank God" as you miss each other and mean the words for the first time in awhile. Get mad when she flips you off, that single red fingernail dancing like devil's fire through the safety glass. Doubt seriously if she will tell her therapist about that.

If you had became entwined, an add-on part of that internal combustion engine, flesh and grey matter mixed with brake fluid like scotch and soda, would you wake up in the stories of your children? Would they speak of playing HORSE or burnt toast?

Hear the voice on the tape again. It says "things change."

Think, "no shit Sherlock." Hear him say, "Some we control, some we are controlled by. But it is the evidence of the present, not the absence of union that makes you feel delight and despair in the very same moment."

You remove the tape from the dash, toss it out the window and watch as a teenager driving a lowered '95 Toyota Corolla with a wall of bass speakers runs over the tape. Hear Puff Daddy rapping his way into the hearts and minds of mindless kids.

Hum a song that comes from one of your past lives, *"Come gather round people and please hear the call..."* Wish you could gather round something other than who you are at that moment in time.

Hear the cell phone. It is your mother calling to ask what you are wearing to Tally's opening. She wonders if she should wear pants and comfortable shoes. Or will this give off the wrong message?

Cringe at the thought of it all. Weep for somebody's future—weep for yourself. You cannot take it anymore. Take, taken, took, tooken...to take, isn't that a verb, an action requiring personal choice?

Feel the tears fall onto your new beige rayon skirt and wonder if they will dry leaving little rings of salt.

Arrive at work feeling fragmented, like your body is not connected to your mind. Wonder if the self-help tape would have addressed that problem on side two.

Walk to your desk knee deep in an ever-expanding cube farm and see the pictures of your kids peeking out from under the memo from the new V.P. of Marketing, the guy with doll hair implants, detailing new regs about camera-ready art. Bend a business nod at the boss as he walks by, quickly picking up the phone and shuffling papers. Capture a large breath and punch the numbers on the phone with false vengeance. They are your dad's numbers. Hang up when a strange voice answers. Remember your father has been dead for 3 years.

How hard can it all be? You have it all but you have nothing.

Just castles made of sand. And you forget who sang that line.

Go to lunch with a fellow worker and listen to her tell you how she regularly "buys" new dresses from Nordstrom's, wears them once to a party and then returns them on Monday.

Picture yourself doing that, but then breaking down at the cashier's counter and admitting that you did in fact wear the dress. Without panties, no less.

You went there clean and got dirty. It's never the same. Just a matter of degrees.

Wonder if you cry too much.

Or not enough. Feel exposed, raw as a December oak.

Drive home, cars swarming, little baby birds waiting for a worm, an opening to get on the freeway, this vein carrying metal and glass objects toward two points converging on the horizon into nothingness, a perspective drawing without prospect.

Pull into the driveway. Are you home or in transit? Open a bottle. Open the mail. Close the window. Close your eyes. Recall a fellow worker saying you looked "spun." Realize that you are not sure exactly what he meant. Come to think of it, you know exactly what he meant.

Stare out the window, comfortably numb as a feeling moves down your skull like warm motor oil. Begin to realize that nature is only out for survival. Contentment and piece of mind take work.

Think about the time in college you made love with a lifeguard in his tower one night. Afterward you asked him what he was going to be when he grew up, like you had a right to know.

Recall how he looked at you oddly, his eyes seeking purchase, and then smiled so sweetly, those saving eyes burrowing their way deep within his thoughts. He said nothing and pointed out to the reflection of the full moon on the water.

Later, he told you that on the edge of land, when the suburbs have chased you to the final sandy cul-de-sac, all you have to do is step in, out and finally, off.

Flick on the new flat screen box and surf the

channels. Ask yourself, can real surfing be any farther apart from watching TV? *Malibu Barbie, Baywatch, Survivor*—this balanced diet for the vicarious, stuck of their own volition, your own choice. Feel like putting your finger down your throat to vomit every "Arco-some people care" commercial ever fed the masses. Stop at the History Channel and see a former box office draw "hosting" a special on the deadliest weapon of the Middle Ages, the crossbow. Fall asleep with face cream dripping on your pillow, your husband's work clothes piled in the corner, feeling middle aged.

Have a dream that you are a champion archer, hitting the center with every arrow you let fly, impaling each previous arrow from the back while a well disguised Robin Hood looks on from behind a tower. Wake up embarrassed but a little satisfied about what you and Robin of Loxley had done, how your subconscious had brought you up against realities, to stand vigil and choose a life for yourself. In your dream he had asked you what does an arrow pierce but wind? You said "fish." He said "hearts."

Something inside you is different this new day. Maybe it's the coffee. Maybe you'll get a letter from Ed McMahon because, "You may have already won!"

Have a conversation with your daughter on the way to school. Well, not really a conversation. For her, you are a ride, a lady in the background with a credit card. Your daughter yanks everything out of the glove box looking for a pen. Napkins and straws and a dead flashlight and a pair of now-out-of-style sunglasses you lost 3 years ago and old McDonald's ketchup packets fall all over the floor of your car. You pray that a bit of what you tell her will seep in, no deeper than a blade tracing figure eights in the ice—infinity signs. You love her, she hates you. You hate her, she loves you. But there are not yet words for that crossroads feeling.

"What is all this shit?" she asks. "Maps, honey," you

tell her very calmly, "Not really places but just ink on a page."

She scrunches up her overly made-up face and asks you if you have been smoking crack.

Try to recall what the word prodigal means, what status quo could ever stand for, why you can't remember which side your gas tank is on after owning this car for 5 years?

Stop to get that gas after dropping her off, run inside to pick up a bottle of aspirin, over-the-counter wine and salt-less pretzels. Reach for the new *Cosmo* but set it down, not knowing why. Be amazed as an elderly man in a uniform holds the door for you, smiles an authentic smile and asks you—no, he doesn't tell you—he *asks* you to have a nice day.

You say nothing, leave, but something pulls you back and now your hands on the steering wheel in that perfect two and ten position are in control of your head which is connected to your heart by strings. Like a puppet. Like fishing line. Like stays for a mast.

Return to find him hosing down the asphalt, humming a Spanish folk song. Walk up to him, tense, tenuous, and speak in a cracking voice through red lips tasting dripping mascara, "thank you," you say, "Gracias."

Ask him his name. In broken English he says, "Jesus." Figures. Give him yours. "Candice-not-Candy," the words melding together as one. Drive away feeling like Mother Theresa. Lighter, almost airy.

Hold that thought, hold it so tight, squeeze it and bring it close inside. Make it your center for the rest of the day, your own private transaction with someone with a name badge that read "Jesus."

There are more of those jewels hidden beneath the TV dinners and raging billboards and this umbrella of Happy Gilmore zeitgeist. You know that now or at least know that you need to know.

To know: That everything is true, but nothing is true,

that the best, they die young, but they live twice, that the trouble with normal is that it only gets worse. That choreography belongs in dance, not out here in the world. That the grainy, unpeopled rawness of life is the texture that all artists hope to capture.

You know that everything just falls into the sea, eventually.

You hold out hope that there must be a wheel's hub someplace from which you can begin to attach stainless steel spokes; wires, roads, people and maps of truth; red bricks, yellow bricks, dirt and rocks that won't crumble in your hand; a compass with character; ladders, handles, lovers...life.

No. It's not easy being you after you have been you.

All you want is a path that begins at the center. That's all, just a place to move out from, like a drop of blue/green paint on a spin art canvas. Like those concentric circles flowing from that skeptic rock thrown in a deeper pond; a wide open horizonless sea.

That's all.

Journaling Out: The Accidental Memoir

"We, the survivors have an obligation to the dead, to remember. And with what is left of our lives, to try to bring goodness and meaning to this life."
Charlie Sheen, *Platoon*

J.D. was struggling; life had become an imposition on him. There were days when it was night before he realized that the day had passed him over. It was the sickness of habit, I'd decided; it was separating him from himself.

And J.D.'s sin was that he smiled all the way down.

I remember that year. It was the Year of the Snake, a Chinese leap year. I finally met my brother through his writing journal; the way it moved and shaped itself in sync with the boiling memories, the way it stood queerly in the well-lighted corner of my study-turned-self-examination skunk works. That was the year I read those hand-scrabble pages backwards as if it was Lennon's, *A Day in the Life*, spun counterclockwise, hoping to hear some answers to the questions we all wished someone would've asked.

It was like that, it's still like that. It will forever be like that. Pain is an ugly dog and the dead take something with them when they go. I know this from his journal, not from reading it but feeling it as if the blue-ink words were synapses in my own brain.

My brother was a silent, still-life drama with raging dissonance penned behind his pallet. He was a stealth neurotic, only acting out the haunting noirs and the tragic comedies after he'd put his kids to bed and opened his bound journals to cut veins and dip his quills into the red-blue blood. Nobody read them. His wife thought he was working on spreadsheets for tomorrow's breakfast meetings.

When she dumped them on my front porch that day, right after the funeral, eyes still puffy and thick, silicone straining against a rayon blouse, all she could say was, "Here, you keep them. I don't understand them. Hell, John, I guess I didn't understand *him*."

"But maybe you could, you know, gain some insight into why...," I asked.

"Ah, c'mon, John. Why does anyone jump off the bridge? He left me all alone, embarrassed me. Why didn't he just do something simple, like have an affair or get hooked on cocaine? Things everybody does; acceptable and correct. And the bridge, for Christ's sake? With TV cameras and rush hour traffic? He could've asked for attention in other ways."

"I think he did." I was holding it together, but only barely.

"He never asked me, never told me. His mystery was my undoing. I could never tell if what he was doing was the right thing for us."

"The right thing indeed, Francine. Too much of the right thing, maybe." I realized that she didn't get it, that I could only make it worse.

"How are the kids, Francine?" I switched subjects.

"I don't know, John. Maybe those writing books of his will tell."

"Francine," I asked as she stomped away, "What do we see when we go blind?" She wrinkled up her nose and only turned part way around, silent, brooding, glossing over her sadness with glitter and rouge. "We see what we should have imagined all along," I called after her. "Don't blame my brother, lots of people become victims of themselves." And she was gone, herself a victim, the former spouse of the formerly wounded idealist, burning rubber in her 735i.

They sat in the file boxes all that summer, talking to me but not very loud. I couldn't put them away and I couldn't read them. They were like palace guards standing sentinel against my own self pity. When a seemingly healthy young man decides to end his life before what everyone thinks will be his apex, you don't celebrate it as you would a normal death.

But what is a *normal* death anyway? People die, normally. But their death, along with their birth, is probably the most unique part of their life.

It was a sultry, late August afternoon when I sweat out that revelation. I had caught myself dialing J.D.'s old office number, wanting to ask him about the betting line on the 49ers or if he wanted to take the kids to the park on Sunday and wear tie-dye. One time his secretary answered and told me that, "Mr. Dorn is no longer with us." And for the slightest of moments, I thought I might've dreamt his death and he had simply changed jobs. It was time to read his journals.

My head could no longer remain a refuge, a shelter for how things should've or shouldn't be. I had to know why so that I could get back to that comfortably numb place where all my brain had to do was process information. I reached for one of the dozen dusty books that spilled over the top of the old box, not knowing or caring if there was any order or clarity. I know that pain changes our lives, not fluffy bunny rabbit moments. What I wanted to know was how do things get so perfectly tragic that a thirty-four-year-old man with two young kids and another forty good summers lining up in front of him can step off the edge of one of the most photographed testimonies to man's dreams? Maybe J.D. just stopped dreaming.

And that's how it started—simply by wondering. I read a few passages, scratched my head, jotted down a few thoughts. Within a week I was digging gopher holes in my mind. By Labor Day, J.D. and I were having imagined conversations about the various aspects of the writing journals. I'd started my own memoir of sorts to test drive this self-aggrandizing. But when set up against J.D.'s boney sinew of armchair revelations—as pathos-laden as they were—I felt like something pathetic was colliding with the truth. It wasn't heroic, not even like brothers trying to bury childhood differences; it was as if separate heartbeats were trying to find one another in the dark, each too weak to sustain themselves alone.

My wife suggested that talking to myself like this was a sign of mental illness. I told her someone was listening. Her eyes gathered something like pity but more like sorrow. I'd seen this before but not in her.

I went to a therapist. He told me to come back every Thursday. I went to a "healer" down by the Wharf, she told me that my friend was "channeling" and gave me the number of a past-life specialist. As I walked back to my car I could see the bridge's frowning arc through the haze. Mocking me.

The first time J.D. actually wrote in my own journal, using *my* hand as his vehicle of choice, "channeling" I suppose, it was early fall and the leaves had covered the back lawn. My wife had left a note on the answering machine before she'd gone off to some conference where they, well...where they confer about things. Her perfume filled the kitchen all day.

"John," her high pitched voice caused the dogs to bark, "Time to put your self back into the race. J.D. would want you to be focused. Can you focus on the yard while I'm gone?" The words, "your self" was spoken with a pause. It was grammatically misused, so I paid it no heed.

Why is it that people can so easily place thoughts into the minds of the deceased? Is it because they can't defend themselves? I'd ask J.D.

J.D., I wrote in my journal, framed as a query, "Did you find yourself trusting your imagination more than your memory, events more than eventuality, your dreams more than what has passed for reality? Because I'm finding that's no way to write in a journal, no way to face the truth that must emerge like a lanced boil that is painful even to the thought but when cut and dripping red paste into a bucket of words and phrases, it feels like no release has before or ever could again, unless, of course, you continue to bury the future as it unfolds and a new infection grows under your skin. And then you write it again…not because you know how but because you can. Did you find that, little brother?"

Heritage-plundering is a learned skill. That's all he said as my finger wrote out his response in blue ink on white space and I mouthed the words quietly behind the closed door.

"Do you remember those months before you jumped even before they began?" I wrote, wondering who I was asking—like a child recalls Baby land, their in-vitro village images that might have happened and might've not? "The pressure must've been building, slowly, then, once it was decided, a sense of the sexually-equivalent urgency put your ass in the chair at night, a pen between your fingers."

Restraint and patience were required, he wrote back in my journal sometime around Halloween, *not the immediacy of wham-slam fulfillment. For the experience of memoir is the way of self-hypnosis—equal parts skill, commitment, subconscious truths, pain, revealment, revilement, nostalgia and if done right, more pain—slow, beautiful, exposing hurt.*

"But little brother," I responded right away, "a journal has to have a beginning but can have no end. When it does, it's called biography or obituary. And then it's written by someone else. What catalyzes the pen though, can be something profound, don't you think? Did you ever feel…profound?"

But, John, you see, that blanket statement is easily

shot full of jingoistic shrapnel. It rarely happens that way. In fact, there is no blank formula for beginning a journal, a memoir or streaming thoughts on a cocktail napkin. For every writer, there is a purpose, under heaven (remember—from bible school, from the song?). I guess I wasn't writer-enough to know where it was taking me. Keeping a journal didn't teach me to say that, it just gave me the courage to lie first and then tell the truth, which, now that I think about it, is the foundation for most good journaling. You lie in your head to yourself about your life and the way it has unfolded, and then you begin to lie on paper, but in the process, the lies fall away with the pretense and slowly, indefatigably, the truth comes out. And when it emerges, as it did with me in that year before I left, you might not recognize it at first. Truth hurts. Humans suck. We suck. I suck. Say it because if you don't, you might as well write fiction where a different kind of truth can be told.

Eliot told it when he said that, "Between the idea and the reality, lies the shadow." In those months before J.D. left, it was dark much of the time. Not black but gray. And the words, the words became moonlight and the worse times were in those long shadows that split the time between sundown and moon rise. We didn't talk, not like we are now. Why didn't you say that things were thick and muddy, I wanted to ask him. And, well…consequential?

Oh, John, but I did. But no one saw, no one noticed through the quiet noise of their own little cat's feet. I don't like gray and don't appreciate ambiguity. I hate those shadowy memoirs that don't even hint because they're too blatant. They only lie; damn romance novels rife with true imagination but false memory, safe-at-any-speed texts with a narrative arc that reads live a flat line EKG. I guess my sign language was more than six degrees from top-dead-center.

When I read this now, it scares me. I know he was right, that pain is the treason of the affected, that all those best-selling homogenous props and postulated preempted strikes for re-elections and movie releases and the general malaise of a sagging super-star ego; all those bad memoirs steal from the raw text of a real life. Even if it's a banal one.

"But J.D., I have to know. Isn't silence the final symptom of despair? You were writing up until you flew and then floated. Your life was not cursory. You were inclined. It says so right here—*I will not let life hammer me into a solid, common shape."*

J.D. didn't write me back until just before Christmas. And during that autumn lull my journal began to take its own shape as an oral history of the subject matter, a collection of individual's anecdotes and a subjective layman's explanation of why, why did he jump? I was using other's words as foundation before I could build my own. And I realized that it wasn't so much mockery as it was muddled diatribe. "He was a good man," "Such a shame," and "Who would've guess it?" As I felt that subconscious need welling up, I was afraid that if I put a label on it, called it *my journal, my answers,* people would ask "Why should I be so obsessed? It was his decision."

But as the words came and the narrative arc steepened into peaks and valleys that directed the text away from the expository and situated them into a leading role of exploration, I began to realize that if I didn't try to disguise or pretend, my own words would find their way to the other side.

While I waited, I began to devour other memoirs, swallowing these polished publications half a dozen at a time. Some had moments of stinging irony and tragic mirth. Others appeared showy, scripted and well-timed, glorified advertorials. The best didn't require me to effort-mine what nuggets lay below the subjective rants and thinly veiled efforts at social posturing. Their personality came through breezily, and you could love them or hate them and everything in between. Behind your back, they challenged you to take a stance, commit to your own feelings toward the writer as subject and the subject as proffered by the writer.

A good memoir would engage. The journal underneath it must've hurt, must've been some fiery, private transaction, a war with oneself where everyone wins. A place where you bring your own redemption because you've mined it by hand; dried blood under the fingernails and all.

The worse ones really pissed me off. "What happened?" I wanted to ask. "Did you find comfort in the shadow of illusion because the dark frightened you?" What genre is this, fairy tale? Science fiction? Docu-denial? It's not even myth because the only lesson here is the degradation of a reader's intelligence, a frightening trend that has not enough value to project beyond a shake of the head. The archetype is banality; forgivable because they're human. Unforgivable for the same reason. It's okay to be a crash test dummy with a typewriter, I wanted to tell them. But that was only part of the self-rhetoric of my convincing. Lord, don't let me fail to engage.

Journal-keepers are writers. And writers are killed for being alike, always the same, always unremembered. But you don't write the true journal to be remembered. The false ones write it to forget their true past and invent something like reality-recollection, where imagination and The Bachelor meet Divorce Court and Judge Judy goes on Jerry Springer to speak of her addiction to pain killers just to disguise her nymphomaniacal conquests. Some call it memoir but it's really just self-flatulation.

The best do it for clarity; not to hide or morph the weakness but to expose its underbelly and rise above the roar on the wings of self-lacerating revelations. Sometimes you apologize for shit you didn't even pull because you certainly thought about, certainly could've done it. And damn, you sure would've enjoyed it. J.D. had said he thought his wife was classes above him. But that's as far as he went.

I wondered about the difference between a journal and a memoir, about the difference between J.D. and me, about being dead and being undead. That was when I realized that J.D.'s words, as much as I missed the mouth from which they came, were no zero-sum game.

I had almost put his voice away and filed the journals on a shelf when he came again on Christmas Eve. I had finally stopped calling his office and his wife had not called me back at all.

You want to know, don't you, brother? The words on my books were clues; the answers are in the white space between them, in that space between where you and I used to move around each other like opposing magnets. Was the unyielding gravity of my options so dismal that I had to practice my jack knife from four hundred and fifty feet instead of at the YMCA high dive? Well, that year before I left, if it was a fish, I'd still throw it back because it deserves to be with its own kind. Other years that were spent dreaming or walking the thin green horizon or rehearsing my own demise, all that was just tired laughter. The fact is, the journal might be written during a certain presence but it also leaks into the future carrying the past along with it. You do it right and you don't have a choice. The surviving reader might perceive it as a snapshot of the person's life but a good journal will speak to the author's dead grandparents and their unborn children. It will be sawed off syntax, a primal necessity only understood by those who might've jumped too, unless they could write their own obituary, tear it up and go home whistling a smart tune.

I tried, big brother, I really tried. We'll talk again in the spring when the yellow mustard coats the hills where we would ride our Schwinns. You keep writing. I like what I'm seeing. Because, John, I can hear your heart from here.

I don't regret the things that I missed that year after J.D. left. What was lost was gained in other ways. I came to know my brother, to know myself, if only between the tattered leather covers. It was a start.

I do regret some of which was cut from the text by my own hand. I can justify it by realizing that people would've been hurt. But what is justifiable narrative, let alone a validated life, if the human condition in all its tainted pleasures and aesthetic tragedies can't be exposed as a collective? There was that one line from one of our last journals, "we give it together, we take it together," I don't remember the context but only how it fits now, staring at me in the rear view mirror asking questions I already know the answers to; things I learned that year.

The words that were erased while I learned not to, like scenes from an over-edited movie, don't mean that they weren't played out in celluloid or life; it just means you don't get to share them. It's not right or wrong, it just is.

Still, as honest and deft as a writer can be, who are they to say, "That's the way it was?"

And yet, if respect and integrity are foregrounded, and research is thorough, is permission necessary? Maybe we have to first give ourselves permission to cut our own vein before we bleed on others. If you write a memoir that makes your family squirm, then you've likely succeeded. Right, J.D.?

It was nearly summer, almost a year since he'd been gone. Then he came back.

Yeah, I remember that last journal, its intimate and subtle joys of the loveliest misery. And wish I could live it again, write it differently. So wonderful was the pain, so beautiful the open scars that I stared thinking they'd heal if I just kept writing. Lots of "ifs," John, not enough "when's." But you're doing okay, I see. You've learned much. And you want to keep writing beyond what we have here? You want to tell the stories of others who can't find their own voice? It's no fun dying and waking up in the stories of our heirs.

"Well, J.D., who am I to say that everything is contextual, that one life's bad joke is another's embarrassment? But yes, the writing is connecting me to parts of myself that I'd become separated from. Look what it did for us? I think that at worst, the memoir runs roughshod over lives without regard for feeling and place; the author's lives first to go on record, and then the names are named. At best, it is brutally honest, but honest still, as honest as any memory can be. Both are necessary. We are not islands. We are a species that favors togetherness over otherness. How can one man's story be told unless it is told in context to another being, another animal, another piece of the earth and all its gifted elements?

"Do you ever wish that you'd written other characters into your journal," I asked him?

I did, John. It was your story. I just never got a chance to finish it.

Do you ever wish you'd graduated from journal to memoir?

Of course, but I never made the transition, never made the jump.

"I can do that for us," I spoke into the mirror, "I can cross that bridge."

Spare Changing

"Once upon a time you dressed so fine. You threw the bums a dime in your prime. Didn't you?"

Bob Dylan, 1965

The day he went off to college, the boy found a note from his first stepfather, written on his best stationery, telling him to make him proud, to do what he would do. There were two crisp $100 dollar bills with the note. The boy had been ready to leave for some time but stayed, mostly because he could. A dorm room would be much smaller than his room at home.

That morning, he climbed into his early model Toyota 4X4, neatly pressed pants in the back and a bag of dope under the seat. The mother stood on the fine porch of their colonial home, halfway between the plaster columns and her son. She stood halfway between what was and what could never be again.

The mother seemed as if she was about to say something important and the boy looked away for a second, giving her room to compose her thoughts. When he turned again, she had gone back inside.

The son walked toward the front door but was halted by the sound of a Doors tune straining to make its way out of the well manicured, well furnished estate.

"Keep your eyes on the road and…"

He climbed into the truck and mouthed the words, "I'm on my own," trying the reality on for size. And then drove away.

They didn't speak for three months. He loved her deeply.

There could be no other way.

The boy's mother was a hippy. She lived through, even thrived in, that strange, confusing, and wonderfully tumultuous period commercially known as "the '60s." The marches, mayhem, she was that flower child dancing to the muse of the music, living in a VW bus, burning incense, peppermints, and her bra. She'd been at the Monterey Pop Festival, got arrested in People's Park, and believed with her whole heart that her generation could change the whole world.

Sometimes the son wished he'd been born a few years earlier, so he could've stood beside her in Grant's Park, May of '68, at the Democratic National Convention, eyes watering from mace. Or born a few years later, the whole thing reduced to a later chapter in a sociology text and a genre of music that goes around.

And comes around.

Four kids, two husbands, a hip replacement and thirty years on a cul-de-sac—it was hard for him to believe, damn, his mom saw Janis live.

At some point it ended for her, as it did for most kids with big ideas, little staying power, and parents in Chicago who'd take them back with only minor limitations. One day she was stoned, living in the Haight that was tripping on itself from its own fame. A few months later she was walking down the steps of the "L," returning to the safe brick and mortar of her Evanston bedroom. A generation was tired.

None had been unaffected.

Seven months after she'd come back, six months before the peace treaty would finally be signed in Paris, she'd given birth to the boy, the result of a transient seed.

But a bastard son was beyond minor limits of discretion and soon enough they were back on the road, trying to bend time. "We-can-do-it-on-our-own," she'd say, tasting and swallowing every syllable.

* * *

It was a Sunday, midway through the fiscal year, more than midway up the corporate ladder, less than halfway through my life. The sky had a nervous feel, the air hung in an unpeopled rawness, and the March wind whistled a strange song.

One hand held car keys and a leather wallet, the other a leather leash that held my chocolate Labrador, Pele. That was my excuse anyway, why I couldn't reach into my pocket to pull a buck out for the haunting figure whose look asked for change.

I had seen this man before, or others like him. They had become part of the urban landscape, like the sounds of ambulances and jackhammers making room for a Banana Republic, a Gap, or another American bistro with little twinkling lights for the nouveau riche. Most of these people carried small cardboard signs. Sometimes the sign's message was a request, other times just a reminder. The words never fixed blame but the reader passing by must've known that something was wrong. Or at least not very right.

Each time I'd passed this one man, or a similar person, I could feel my stomach turn. His sign had said he was a vet. I believed it and put off the rumble in my gut to bad cappers on last night's angel-hair pasta and vowed to choose another twinkling bistro the next time.

I really didn't care if he'd served his country, was an alcoholic looking for a freebie, or just some guy who'd convinced himself that he was an actor waiting to be discovered. Here he stood on a street corner with his dark, enveloping stare and his sign, and I was walking a half block away to shell out three bucks for a cup of designer coffee. Welcome to America, man. Yeah, survival of the fittest and all that sociology crap.

The man was wearing a dirty denim jacket, torn gray pants that showed one pale, hairy knee, and high-top tennis shoes laced only to the ankle. The bottoms had been re-soled with matching duct tape. It was his shamelessness that moved me, not the cammie-green beanie pushed back on his squarish head, or the tail end of a scar peeking out and traveling towards his left eye. He had the forehead of an older college professor or maybe a ship captain, with deep-set lines running vertically toward the heavens.

As Pele and I came up on him, he stood his ground, a proud dime-store-Indian-like figure with thick fingers and a cupped hand, whispering and grunting at the passersby. He made no sudden or jumpy movements but people gave him a wide berth, as they would a Doberman or a Jehovah's Witness. One of my eyes read the sign asking for help. The other avoided it.

"Sure bud," I said in a momentary wave of philanthropy. "But my hands are full. I'll catch you on the way back." We exchanged looks. Maybe he said something. Maybe I didn't hear it.

My stomach moved again and my dog sat down at the man's feet, staring off into the busy street. The man reached down to pet him, looking where my dog looked.

"C'mon Pele," I said, wondering what they saw. "Let's get some coffee."

By the time Saigon fell in '75, the mother had traded a part of her spirit for stability, traded the road for a Republican. You'd like to think she mortgaged her rebelliousness for the boy's future, not quite selling out, but selling short. "It'll-be-so-great-son-with-a-roof-over-our-heads-and-the-cops-not-hassling-us."

He was a good man, gentle and diligent, good at commerce, a man who put on his turn signal 100 yards before the corner. He loved the mother matter-of-factly, even if he didn't understand her. When he took the boy to his office, he introduced him as his son. The mother, well, she seemed happy enough.

Inside the Starbucks I was overcome by an unfamiliar nausea and a pain that rested just behind the veil of my sunglasses. It was the hollow longing in his eyes, the vacant stare of missed opportunities. I'd seen it in older men passed over for promotion, but in the street it was different. The plea from his cardboard sign repeated itself in my mind: Homeless Vet Needs Help, Homeless Vet Needs Help, Homeless Vet...

I ordered my latte, handed the lady a twenty, and wondered about the fates that placed us where we are—a can of beans for him, a fresh raspberry scone for me. How did it get the same as it ever was? An anonymous feeling took hold and moved out from the center like spin art, a faceless enemy. I felt like I was living in someone else's tragic play, a mettre-en-scene.

I went over to the window to check on Pele and looked up to the corner to where the man had been. My dog was still looking in that direction as well. But I couldn't see the man or his sign and was struck by a weird image of a dog autopsy proving that the inside of a dog's body is mostly heart. A few small entrails, a liver and whatnot—but the heart would take up the rest.

Take it easy, Pele, I thought. I tried to quiet something inside myself that was moving quicker. We'll go to the park later.

Dammit, didn't they have VA benefits? Some kind of shelter? It seemed to me, although I didn't remember well, that my mother and I had spent a few nights in a converted high school gym when it was too cold for the bus. We had probably stood in soup lines too, she in a long hand-me-down coat, me strapped to her back, watching, waiting, head buried in her long, beaded braids. "They-can't-sabotage-our-hope-son-they-can't-take-that-away." I tried to block the feeling, but the effort only engaged it more. I searched for a description of what I was feeling. All I knew was that it was woven of my past and future and my own pathetic little human heart.

The girl behind the counter called my name. I ordered another coffee to go, large with sugar and cream, and three blueberry muffins. I put the coffee and the muffins in a bag, added the change and a few extra bills, and walked out into the street, a hand for Pele, a thought for the past.

My mother had grown up, I grew up; items checked off her growing lists. There were grocery lists written on envelopes, housecleaning lists written on the backs of receipts, an eclectic collection of to-do's and will-do's and must-do's scattered from the oak front door to the attic and beyond.

Pick up cleaning.

Bathe the dog.

Call Grandpa on his birthday.

Check out sale at Montgomery Ward.

One day I found a different list, a short, obscure, and boldly fonted collection of phrases in a leather journal buried in the bottom drawer, just below her clean socks, motherly bras, and a paisley scarf I'd never seen her wear.

Make a difference, one said. *Anxious to matter*, said another.

The homeless guy had drawn a peace sign on the bottom of his cardboard sign. Or was it a button from his jacket? I wondered if he had watched the NBA playoffs. Did he have family somewhere? A mother with a list? Or had he been crossed out?

Here's a baby boy. Maybe he was born to unfortunate circumstances. But he's a living, breathing creature, not a doll or a nightmare or an abortion. Maybe his cards were stacked against him from the beginning. Or maybe he screws up along the way, makes a few kid-mistakes that escalate. And no one steps in to help, to shake him up or give him a break or just talk to him on a hot Saturday afternoon.

The kid grows up thinking that life ain't fair. Maybe the rest of us know it, but we don't have it rubbed in our faces every day by absent mothers and abusive drunk dads and parole officers and other punks who hang with us, spreading their own disease of submission.

And one day, a kid like this just says, "fuck it." Maybe he robs a liquor store and goes to jail. Or he's shot dead. With some luck maybe he joins the army in a last gasp at life.

Suddenly I realized the power the homeless vet held and I wanted to ask him for forgiveness, absolution, for having three cars in my garage and enough athletic shoes to outfit a small town in Nebraska.

I wanted to ask him if he had the answers to the questions that the preacher at my well-dressed church never seemed to ask. What is the difference between a cloud of *Amen*s and a bottle in a paper sack? They serve the same purpose, don't they? Some kind of attempt at finding validation or search for purpose? Or just a momentary sculling for peace, if not redemption. What follows unfulfilled faith and hope? More faith and hope, or a gradual slither down into coping?

And then just surviving?

When I arrived back at his corner perch, he was gone. Where could he have gone? I wondered. I told him I'd catch him on the way back, didn't I? Did he think I would lie? Now who was going to look me in the eye and say it was okay, take the hot coffee with half-mittened hands, gaze into the white paper bag, smile yellow broken teeth and bless me?

I put Pele in the backseat of my SUV and began to drive up and down alleys looking for the man, cursing myself and cursing him.

Before he'd left for school, had thought his mother, Mary, was typical—another dreamer trying to turn value into abundance. At the dinner parties though, when the wine uncorked stories of '68 and '69, he realized she would forever struggle with the balance of human tenderness and legal tender. He knew that paisley scarf would rise again, if only to grace their dog's collar.

He had seen the old photos of her and read the letters she had written to his grandparents. There were letters from before his existence and after she'd come and went. It was funny to find himself like a bookmark in her letters, to see that he had so much bearing on the nature of things.

June '69: Mom and Dad: It's great to be out here on the coast and I'm OK. Yeah, I really am. I don't have much money but seem to always get what I need. People look out for each other, enough that I feel somehow connected. I'm not sure to what, but I feel whole, if you can understand that. Please don't try and find me. Peace, Mary.

I thought of what I would ask him, and in my mind I started a list of things he might need, but then I stopped. A lot of people needed a lot of things. A lot of people pulled themselves up and made it against tough odds.

How had he become trapped in this scene, when other kids from his neighborhood were holding good jobs instead of a cardboard sign? Maybe they were living narrow lives with wide wallets but they sure as hell weren't relying on the sympathy of others for a meal. What was his version of this age-old tragedy? Did he feel like a character from dark play? How tough was tough?

My mother, Mary, had worked at a hospital and for that period, spoke words of wisdom. I don't think she got paid for it. It was a mental institute and she scolded my sister and me when we called it a funny farm. One time I heard her speaking to my stepfather about the men who had fought in the war. It didn't make any sense, she'd said, they didn't seem like old war heroes. They weren't even twenty-five and they'd seemed as if they'd lived two lifetimes. And then, as I remember thinking, they were told that they were sick in the head.

As kids, we'd played army, even pretended to kill our friends when we caught them out on the street. When we got sick we stayed home from school. Never had to go to a funny hospital.

Aug. '71: Dear Mom and Dad: I had a job at a clothing store for a few months but I didn't like having to sell people stuff they didn't need. Some people are doing some weird things these days. I know this sounds funny, but I trust the people, just not the things. We are living in a house most of the time and your grandson is learning to walk. I'm worried about the stairs though, like you used to, Mom. But I feel safe in the park, even at night. Love, Mary.

What if I never saw him again? What if he OD'd that night? But I doubted a man like this would kill himself. It would be below him. Dying would be easy. Living is the challenge, isn't it? That's another thing I'd ask him.

"Were you afraid?" I'd ask.

"Always," I imagined his response, "it stays with you like a permanent rash. Like a bloodstain on the carpet that soaks right through to the foundation, through to the earth. Dust to fucking dust. And you! What do you want from me? Some sort of downloaded truth?"

He'd look at me, I pictured, his eyes scanning for any sign of authenticity, his big rough hands rubbing Pele's chin softly. Then he'd ask me what I was afraid of.

"You," I'd tell him. "I'm afraid of you."

"Yeah, I'm a scary fucking metaphor, aren't I? You're afraid of what I represent." And Pele would bark at the night.

Just that morning I'd been sitting in church with my perfect little family: 2.3 kids, B-level tennis-playing wife, wearing my chinos and pressed pastel shirt, initials monogrammed on the cuff. I sat surrounded by others from the stucco cul-de-sac, like-minded capitalists, disconnected from the human capital. Most of us were there to cleanse something, to ask forgiveness for coveting a neighbor's spouse, a 735i, a corner office. We just wanted a weekly tune-up, a spiritual re-do. We'd tell God we screwed up, generally meaning it. And then sneak in a prayer that our portfolios would ride out any technical corrections.

The preacher had said that the earth was a very small stage in a vast cosmic arena. He'd said that many emperors and generals had led soldiers, shedding blood in that theater only to keep us free.

If I found my homeless vet, talked to him, gave him the coffee, what would my mother think? Was that "making a difference"? Should I take him to her hospital? How would she define freedom?

What would she say if I drove him upstate to their home on the fairway, behind the gate? Would she reach into her husband's wallet? Invite him in? Give him an old coat and flash him two fingers in the shape of a V?

Would she remember?

So what if he'd bought a bottle of cheap wine with the money? In this form of self-medication, the only difference between the *haves* and the *have-nots* is the age of the grape.

Jan. '72: Dear Mom and Dad: Dion got lost today. Someone found him but I was really scared. There were lots of people jumping and screaming in the park. I think the loud music hurt his ears. It gets really cold out here when the wind blows. The lines for food are long but it's free. How are things back home? You know, Dad, he has your eyes...and your ability to make money. He found a five dollar bill on the sidewalk today. Luv ya...Mary and Dion.

The wind kicked up little dust devils as I drove through the fading afternoon avenues. It was blowing me to some place I didn't know or had forgotten, a place that might quietly harbor a stranger with stringy, greasy hair. Just a man, I thought, living a bedeviled existence, in search of one meal of grace from a passerby.

Like communion.

I tried to remember one of the hymns from church but nothing honest registered. I turned on the radio and the Hendrix version of Dylan's, "All Along the Watch Tower" came on. *Plowmen dig my earth.* I turned the volume up and Pele started whining. The loose skin around my waist jiggled against the seatbelt in time with the bass notes.

Then I saw him. He was sitting in an alley against the back wall of a Greek restaurant, slumped over, hugging his knees. I stopped the car. He seemed to be mumbling to himself. Maybe he'd just fallen into that no-man's-land between the rawness of survival and the coded language of fictional satisfaction—the new demilitarized zone that separated the social classes. Pele put her wet nose on the window. She turned to look at me as if to say, I gotta piss.

The mother had been shopping and brought home a dog for the little boy. The stepfather was allergic to dog hair, so the dog had to sleep in the laundry room and then in the garage and finally in the backyard. But she had a nice pad to lie on. One day when the boy was twelve and his mother and stepfather were still away for the day, the boy let the dog out to run and she took off like a jet. The dog stopped at the edge of the driveway, turned her head to look at the boy, and then ran off. She was gone for three days.

The boy was put on restriction by his stepfather, mostly because he wouldn't say what happened. The mother refused to discuss it, even after the little dog came home and she snuck cookies for the dog after the stepfather had gone to bed.

Approaching the man slowly, glass crunching under my loafers, I glanced over at Pele. She was alive with the fresh odors of alley life. I heard the man's self-conversation and looked for the object of his words. But I knew who he was speaking to. He brought his eyes slowly up to meet mine. As I opened my lips to say something, his acid-sweet smile seemed momentarily to clear his head.

No words came. The wind filled my open mouth.

He waved a paper sack at me. "Come my friend, sit," he seemed to be commanding me. So I did, the bullet having been lodged, shot from the gun of all those who forget, aimed at all those who carry defeat for the rest of us. Like somebody's son.

Pele came up and joined us, and I told her to stay, to stay here, girl.

"Why?" he asked, his voice low, raw, and clear.

The best I could do was to say I didn't want her to cut her feet.

His laugh bounced off the building walls. "Then give her your Guzzi shoes." Pele went off in search of something vermin-like and real.

We sat in silence for a moment. I could hear someone speaking Greek, late-model car alarms, a siren in the distance. I heard a wild alley cat growl.

The man leaned in close. He smelled like all the parts of life we try to wash off or mask with makeup, cologne, labeled clothes…lists. He placed a damp hand on my shoulder and then with his other hand threw the bag and bottle hard against the far wall of the alley. Green shards of glass rained down, carpet bombing his home. The purple fluid ran quickly down the alley floor.

I don't recall him looking for a reaction from me. It seemed spontaneous but also like he'd done it before. He observed me like a young psychiatrist.

I wanted to run, to wake from my dream. Instead, I held his haunting stare until something inside me broke. I stood up and walked to my car. Pele stood off to the side, his head moving from him to me like a k-9 metronome. She knew we weren't going anywhere.

I returned with a nice cabernet that awaited yet another dinner party. As I handed him the tall, shapely bottle he tried to laugh, but hacked up a hospital sound from his chest.

"My, my. What shall we do?" he asked. "I seem to have left my corkscrew in the shopping cart."

I took the bottle, shoved the cork down into it with my thumb, and drank powerfully, feeling a chill wind blow up the alley.

His eyes settled on a spot somewhere in the sky. The moon maybe, a star, an empty black nothingness.

"You ever see those pictures they take from them space ships?" he asked. "The earth looks weird, don't it? Just some little globe in the sky. You can't see the people, cuz we're so small or maybe all spread out."

"When I see those pictures," I said, the wine loosening my tongue, "I always think, that's us right there, in the big green area. It's not though, is it?"

He grunted in a funny way. "It might be you out in the backyard, barbecuing, waving at the camera. But I might be sleeping under a bridge, hidden from the cosmic, hidden from the Man who lives up there." The vet took my fancy wine and drank long and deep from it.

"He went crazy for a while," he said, deliberately.

"Who?" I asked.

"You know. That guy who walked on the moon. I heard he was just sitting out in his backyard, looking up at that big ol' yellow moon. Next thing you know he's 5150, all sorts of crazy docs trying to get him right. But I tell ya something for nothing. A couple of nights under the bridge, we'd fix his head. None of us have letters after our name anymore. We never had a PHD but we had a PFC."

Then he began to speak in a rough whisper, like sound moving down a dry creek bed. Something like shame coming up against disgust. "I just don't know how.

I was making it, man. I was doing okay…

"But it's dry under the bridge," the man continued after a long pause and a longer drink, "And there are others like me to talk to, or we talk with ourselves. It ain't so bad, not when the cops leave us alone. Those bastards though, they don't believe me when I tell them I was *there*. There for Tet."

After a while I stood up to leave, stumbled like a baby giraffe then stood again, comfortably numb. I heard the man mumble in his half-sleep, his head cradled in the cave of his arms and I realized that the only way to avoid losing it was to never own it.

But now *I* felt owned, or pawned, by the guy hanging on the wall in the church. How much would it cost to buy myself back? What is guilt but a hangover in disguise?

I could smell food rotting in the alley. "Pele," I called out, feeling deeper into the world, connected to a rope that was tied, maybe to a ladder. Maybe to an anchor. Pele showed up with a huge rat in her mouth, the rodent still struggling to free itself. She looked at me, sensed the disdain, and dropped it at the man's feet.

The man stirred. His slurred, gravelly voice broke the night. "Good boy, Pele. Now just go on home with Dion," he said. "Go on home."

"How do you know my name?"

"You told me."

"I did? Well, what's yours?"

"I'm, uh, Moses. Can't you tell?"

The leather seats in my car felt cold and stiff. I picked up the coffee and muffins and tried to walk a straight cop-line back toward Moses' home for the night. Pele whimpered. Halfway there, I stumbled, fell, and cut my hand on a piece of glass. The coffee and muffins and money spilled out against the back wall of a drycleaners or a barber shop. I didn't know. The letters on the wall were chipped and faded in the dusk. When I stood up my hand was bleeding.

Moses sat up. He waved his hand in front of his face like a cowtail shooing flies, a five-fingered metronome marking time. He looked at the bills and crumbs and made a *tsk, tsk, tsk* sound.

I heard him count and then describe the blood drops falling from my hand, the dim streetlights casting its glow.

The first one looked like a snowflake.

The next like a pitchfork.

The third like an angel.

The last one like a grenade.

Turning to leave, I reached for Moses' hand with my bloodied one. He handed me the bottle with the fancy foreign label and said it was time for him to be scrounging his next meal.

"I can't be tilting at windymills all night," he said. "The frog-wine would go well with anything on a night like this."

Learning to speak French, it had been on her list. She would go to Paris to see Morrison's grave someday.

April '72: Dear Momma and Pop: They're all dead. It's not right. I don't know what happened. I think I'm ill. I need to come home. You're his grandparents. Can you send me bus fare? I'm sorry… Mary.

Pale streetlights came and fell, shedding light, shedding the nothingness of a snake's dead skin. I left that man, Moses, never to see him again in person. But he existed in the face of every man I would ever meet: sometimes as guilt, sometimes as ignorance, sometimes like half-empty bottles of inspiration lying at my feet.

There were times Moses haunted my dreams.

Years later, when he'd mostly faded from the

drop-shadow of others' outline, I ran into another Moses; different corner, different rags, same eyes. Same as it ever was. I gave him a hundred dollar bill. He asked for twenties instead. And I obliged.

That night, tucked under a down comforter on a king-sized bed, my wife asleep, I dreamt that I had been a war hero, marching in a parade to the sound of a high school band playing "Stars and Stripes." Then I was standing on a street corner, wrapped in faded fatigues and a torn wool blanket, wearing a cardboard sign around my neck that read "Sell order at 23?," a little peace sign drawn in the O. And Moses was sitting by a campfire, roasting my dog on a spit made from the sport rack from my SUV. A mother was standing in the background, an American flag headband over her blonde-gray hair, playing a Fender Strat strung upside down with her song list taped to the back. Moses wore army boots made from alligator skin and around his neck was a war medal made of plastic and wax. It had a little spinning arrow on it, like an arrow from a board game that moved in sync with the irregular beating of his heart.

Moses pushed his dirty finger through the middle of the medal and then pulled it back; the hole closed up like water swallowing a stone.

"Look at that," he said to the audience of soldiered trees. "Wounded, not even dead!"

Slicing off a piece of my dog's hindquarter, Moses moved out of the ring of fire, but the fire walked beside him as he limped up to me on the street corner. There was no heat from the fire. No warmth. Only a dim starlight glow from a stage set.

"Take it Dionysus," he said to me, offering the dog while the wax dripped onto the silver fork. And as I did, his skin volume began to heat up, liquid breath now from the blue-tipped flame, and he smiled bright white teeth through cracked and blood-dripping lips as my mom played the national anthem in A-minor. When she was finished, she started to walk away but then returned and unfurled a bedroll.

The smells in the air had colors: yellow for rice, brown for burning flesh, green for cologne, and red, white, and blue for patchouli oil. The fire smelled clean, like wet asphalt after an Easter rain.

A small ember jumped out of the flame and landed on my palm, but there was no pain. That scar as well, healing as the wetness from a living Pele's tongue moved over that place.

Lives are crossed, souls are bent in an intimate mystery. It's all perfectly natural; a naked, constant fate. Perfectly natural. Perfectly tragic.

Are their tales and truths able to just cease to exist? One day they are so real that they cannot even be called real and the next just a strange dream-flow over which little time but much water has passed?

I came from her womb, schlepped like a sack of supplies in those early days, carried from town to town on her long skirted hip, planting seeds that would save me from the desperate depths of prosperity.

And now he was six years old again. And the mother he loved stood on the small wooden porch, the wind hitting her cheeks from both sides now: one a kiss, a cold slap for the other.

And her voice rang into the dusk, "Time-to-come-home-Dion-the-streetlights-are-on."

But the return path was only that—another path to another place, with no direction home. The wind began to howl. He cried into it—Mary!

Men at Play, Boys at Work

I was starting to get that feeling back. I could always tell by the music that I picked out. When I was on a roll, laying pipe like a commercial plumber getting paid by the linear foot, I tended to grab the old jazz stuff: Dizzy, Miles, the Bird, rifts that mellowed me out, kept my rhythm going and my strength up.

But when things slowed down from time to time and I let the boys rest, I went for the upscale, high rent music; classics with no words, dead white guys with fifty-cent names. Downtime was important. You have to keep the boys from working overtime on too many time cards. Otherwise they'll go on strike and ain't nobody gonna get paid in bucks or booty.

But I never let the pool run too low or the boys to gettin' lazy. Damn sure that's what happens to the old men lurking at Lous' bar—they stopped getting it, let the kids go into a deep freeze and those fishy little bastards just never woke up. Pool went dry, plaster cracked. Cost to fix it was too high so they just let the plumbing get old before it needed to be. Shame, if you ask me.

I'd only been out of the joint for a month or so—it's hard to tell—and was in dire need of things: shelter, tooth paste, love...respect. But damn if they all didn't seem the same to me, at some level anyway. I could tell 'cuz I'd been listening to Iron Butterfly's, "In-a-gadda-da-vida," five, maybe four times a day.

But the monkey had swallowed a wrench. Crappy little pot bust tripped me up, a war hero and all. Judge said things had changed in twenty years. I told him I read the papers, knew forty-year-old guys in the Guard who'd been called up to the Gulf War. Told him the thing was bullshit.

He didn't like that, I guess.

Seems to me, I told him, they pretty much the same: neo-coloquialism or colonial some-shit. Less than an O.Z. and I'm doing six months. Wrong place, wrong time. I hate Utah.

But I was back in Chapel Hill after that, where I belonged and was feeling *fully rehabilitated*, as they say. Things was going fine.

Most of the talent that I'd been lining up had come from my job as a pool man. That's how come I know all about alkaline and PhD balance and stuff. At first it was easy, fish-in-a-barrel shit, you know, the fringe benefits. But then guys were writing in to the magazines every month, making up stories about the tuna bringing out lemonade with a fish-shaped condom floating in there amongst the anchor-shaped ice cubes. That was bad enough, but then some limp-dick scientist comes up with those "hard-on pills," so even the stressed-out lawyer husbands who worked like dogs to afford a trophy house and a pool and an under-thirty chick could get it up on command. Like pay-per-view stiffies.

Oh well. As John Cougar said, "Ain't that America."

That's when I got my rainstorm idea.

I was watching this old Tarzan movie with some di-vor-ce' who I was just about ready to give the flick to. Man, she had just gone and bought me a 'lectric shaver. Wasn't even my birthday. What pussy uses a 'lectrical shaver? I wasn't about to be a line item in her lawyer's check book. Splitting VA bennies is like ripping a one dollar bill in half.

So, we were watching this Tarzan thing and the monkey-man's swinging through the jungle and shit and next thing I know the chick's rocking back and forth on my new velour couch.

"Damn, woman," I say, "I don't need no tracks on that velveteen."

She got kinda' quiet but I was still pissed…horney,

but pissed.

"Man, there are *rules* here," I told her. "This ain't the Nam."

Anyway, the next day I got to thinking on this brainstorm and started a tree service. Got me a used chain saw down at Art's Pawn and Pool, some Converse high top climbing shoes and lots of rope. I hired some Mexican kid away from the competition, told him he could be a partner if he got us some gigs and showed me how to tie those fancy trucker's knots.

Within a month we were showing promise. I would go in behind the competition, promise the customer I'd undercut their price and then do my best to whack off a few of the right branches.

Who's to say if a tree is trimmed right proper or not? Far as I can tell, it grows the way it wants. You just show them the pile of branches, look really tried and dirty and mention that you probably underbid the job but you were an ar—teeest who truly loved his work. Others, mostly the guy paying the bill, could be a little auspicious. But I gave 'em an honest day's work, just the same.

Far as I can tell, honesty is as relevant as the size of the pile. It can be paper or problems or pulp—if you're proud of your pile at the end of the day, then at least you're honest with yourself. Even if you're lying.

Soon though, word got around, and with plenty of work, I was able to focus on the potential clientele. No piles here, just plain 'ol poon-tential. Now, the pool business had been easy. You just know that if some rich trim is hanging around the house while you clean her pool, glancing out the window while you brush the tile with the long pole, she ain't exactly leading a fulfilling life. It's your *duty,* should the opportunity arise, to increase the fluid levels of a depressed humanity. Car motors or bodies, things need fluids.

In all my years I only was wrong twice, well, three times if you count that weirdo off of Sunset who was having her boyfriend film us in the Jacuzzi. He tried to convince me I could make a fortune in his line of work. He didn't seem too happy when I poured pool acid on his VCR camera. Bunch of sick fucks. Man has to have some integrity in this life.

Things were good though, my creative genius coming to frutation. First, I made sure Paco knew the drill. I had grown my hair out a bit, took off my shirt and climbed up the tree we were to be trimming. Then I had Paco call the lady of the house out to answer a question. He'd walk her over to a spot below me and I'd say "be careful madam, there's nothing to save me if I fall." Then I'd point out a few limbs stuck up at forty-five degrees that I'd cut the ends off of and shaped with my hand saw.

"Madam," I'd ask real husky-like, "those appendages there, they could turn out to be something else in the spring with care and new growth or they could get blown off in a wind storm. You have any ideas what you'd like to do with them?" It's amazing what a little subliminated advertising will do.

Well, I began averaging about forty percent call-back, and was even making some real dough on the side. Ortiz...or Paco, he was working his own angle on me so I had to shut him up by over-paying the kid. No wonder there's so many Mexican TV channels now. But I liked him and figured his people were here in America before the gringos were.

I didn't like having a partner but I had had a few close calls with dumb-ass husbands coming home for a surprise lunch visit and needed Paco to play watch dog. What are these husbands thinking, anyway? Man, if you're married and you're not sure if your wife is satisfied, never go home at lunch without calling up ahead. There are too many guys like me fixing things.

Anyway, the whole thing came to a crashing blow, as all good things must. Mrs. Dravecky needed her lilac bush trimmed, just a quick thinning and fertilizing, but I was on my way over to the Holsten residence to remove some dead wood and let more light in the house. I thought maybe I'd just give the boys a quick work out first. *No problemo*, as Paco said, *You da real swinging monkey*.

Mrs. Dravecky was something else though. She had me doing the mountain climber yells and everything. "Belay on, climbing down, ready to repel." It was kinda' corny but I figured if you're in the service industry then the customer is always right.

I had got to the Holsten's late on account of the boys were getting a bit tired and Mrs. Willis had wanted me to quickly make sure her sprinkler system was working. We pulled up to the gate and Paco said he was too tired and hungry to work so I slipped him a twenty and set him to chillin' on the front porch until I settled the bill with the client. By then, I knew we'd be itchin' for some rest 'cuz I was starting to listen to country music. One more do-si-do, I told them, and we went to work.

Well, sure enough, Mr. Holsten had forgotten his briefcase and comes driving up the long driveway in his Jagular while Paco is sleeping on the front porch chaise lounge. I don't hear his car because I'm doing my best Tarzan yell, jumping on the bed in this tiger stripe loin cloth the lady had made for me.

What's a professional to do?

I was moving toward the edge and I knew it. So did the boys. They weren't responding quick enough.

"C'mon guys," I pleaded. "Two weeks of Moat's Art if you get this last job done right." Well, they agreed and we got down to business.

By then Mr. Holsten is looking at a sleeping Mexican on his front porch and hearing a bunch of animal sounds coming out of his house. It's a good thing Paco always slept with the chain saw on his lap. I think it slowed Holsten down when he fired it up and waved it in the air like a Chinese Samurai cat.

Inside, Jungle Lady and I were scrambling for air,

knowing that the chainsaw was a signal that the lion had returned to his den.

I went out the back door while his wife told him that the jungle sounds he heard were part of this music that the tree trimming crew used to get in the right frame of mind. The little Mexican had been meditating on that big cypress out front. She told him we were like, Buddhist cutters or something, started telling him we would rid the trees of some mold called fungus shway.

It sounded like a damn good lie, which she had been. I began to respect her for her abilities. Holsten was no dummy though. He simply got back in his car and drove away.

Bad things started to happen to me beginning when his woman, the Jungle Lady, showed up at my apartment door with a big leopard skin suitcase. She was moving in on account of she'd been thrown out. It was my fault so I'd have to put her up for a few days until her lawyer could straighten things out. California Style was the term she used.

Turns out they weren't even married. Shit, they weren't even dating. When I asked her what the hell she was doing at his house she went and tried to hit me. But when I grabbed her wrist, she pulled me in real close and there went the whole afternoon. Dang.

She lived with me for two dysfunctional weeks. We wore each other out and the night I come home extra tired because Paco had missed his first day of work ever, the monkey-woman was gone. Took my Beatle's *White Album* with her too. Funny thing was, I kind of liked her. She coulda' stayed.

Within a month, I'd had my work-truck repossessed, my business license revoked and my climbing boots stolen off my front porch. The morning someone kyped them, I thought about re-enlisting. Then I remembered that I'd need my arms and legs to earn a living after I got back. New kinda' war—they blow shit up but it don't kill you for dead, only kill you for living. Dang.

That's when Holsten pulled up in front of my building in that forest green Jag. The guy left the door open and the motor running. I was sure one of the brothers woulda' jacked it. Christ, he had some balls.

I put on some pants, reached for the Louisville Slugger under the velvet couch and waited for him at the door.

"Are you Jarrell Mailer, the tree trimmer?" He was wearing a four-piece business suit with more buttons than my fatigues.

"All day long, I am." I leaned into the 36-inch piece of oak, my hand wrapping itself around the thin handle.

"I have something for you here," Holsten said, and reached inside his coat pocket while I lifted the bat and stepped back away from the doorway, fuckin' Lou Gehrig on my mind.

I saw an envelope come flying in the doorway and land smooth, spinning like a bottle.

"It's your payment, Mr. Mailer. You know, for the trees." I picked it up and looked inside. There were a bunch of c-notes. I wasn't going to count them right there.

"I don't understand," I started to say but he was already half way to his car. I lifted my hands in gesture from the stairway, "What up?"

"I had required that sort of thinning around my estate," he called out to me while slipping into his leather seats and rolling down the bronze-tinted window. "The place was a veritable jungle." I think he winked at me but I wasn't aroused if you were thinkin' that. And then he drove away, smoothly, signaling at the corners and everything.

I went inside and listened to the building creak and moan.

I'll tell you what—the world's a funny place. I know I'm not the sharpest tool in the closet but I got to make a living same as anyone. People only believe and act like-what they want to. Some other schmo might not have been as gentle. I never stole nothing, always treated them nice. Trees is trees and nature takes its own way with things. Sometimes we're victims of our own fakeness. Others just fake their victimness. You know, like your carma running over your dogma.

I have a buddy, a sparky, a 'lectrician who's really into computers. He has this thing called Photo-shopping. Says he doesn't buy anything because if he can imagine it, he can draw a picture of it and the computer will draw up a small poster for his wall. Then he can dream and save his money until some scientist invents it and a company makes it. He calls it "different gratification."

Can you imagine being Santa Claus these days and trying to fill three billion custom orders? Personally, I don't think people really know what they want. That's why I offer them two or three simple, biological options. I don't see how I'm a bad guy. You want to blame somebody for the likes of me, just turn on your TV. Look for the guy who can convince people to spray paint the bald spot on their head. He's the one who ought to be locked up. Him and the government.

Geez, now Uncle Sam's trading partners with them ghosts from the North. People going there on vacation 'cuz they *want to*. Ho Chi Minh dot com and Punji Sticks-R-Us.

More I think about it, saner I get.

A Requiem Road

I'd almost forgotten about that time…and this story. But that's a lie. It's never very far from the surface; a fiery brew of the pathetic and the empathetic. It's a sweet burn, scorching that past in its wake.

Some days bits and pieces of it, of him, will drip into my conscious as candle wax. But they aren't that hot if I let them set for awhile, safe just knowing that I could scrape them away with my peach finger nails. On other days, he just comes out of the fog and hangs with me for awhile, a ghost asking me to set his soul free by telling the story. I never trusted men-in-white ropes, either real or imagined. They seemed so…airy. But I learned to deal with this one while he rattled around, waiting.

Sometimes he'd bring ghastly friends with him and they'd do his bidding, saying things like, "How many unwanted house guests with your keys do you want?" I'd remind them that they lived in their own dimension not mine.

And we both knew that too, was a lie. Their world might've been different but we existed exactly nowhere. Together.

Then, on a regular day, a Tuesday, not even a Friday, out of the darkest marrow of a quiet conversation came my revelation. Not the undoing of what'd been done, not the death of this ghost, not a repaving of the trampled veldt where my heart had lie down quietly to die slowly. No, it was something naïve and childish and forever. Something larger than real life, born out of two co-workers talking. In the rain.

Driving.

Working for a living.

It was one of those rain-or-don't-dammit days, flaky showers finding their way among large pockets of sun. I told Billy, my young co-driver, just a kid, really, that something was going to happen today. He gave me that "you're a mixed-up aunt" look, said the delivery load was light, the same old places—the Veteran's Hall, a pick-up at the Food Bank, the Catholic church downtown and one other place he'd already forgotten about because it was too close to thinking about getting off of work.

I knew the ghost was there, perched somewhere near the intersection of my past and present. He was alone. And he seemed agitated, like he'd had too much coffee or something. I felt my hands on the steering wheel of the big delivery truck that hauled food for people who needed it and others who didn't but felt the desire for something else that we brought—the thought that there were people left who cared.

My palms were clammy and I was glad for the thick rumble of the large diesel. It drowned out the silence I looked for and the world must've seen the tiny beads of sweat under my old cap as they rose through the chill.

"I got a weird feeling," I told Billy, "like I have to vomit or something."

"Food poisoning?" The kid asked. He had an odd maturity to his manner, a kind of raw and graceful elegance to his wit and in his mostly unrefined approach. Billy was the younger brother every girl wished for, the little boy with so much heart that one way or another you knew that his kindness would kill him in the end.

"Maybe, but it's deeper than my stomach. You can't throw up a bowel or a liver can you?" I tried to humor it away.

"Never read about it happening in the tabloids," he replied, thumbing through an old National Geographic.

"Can't be true then," I said, and told the ghost in my head to settle down.

But Billy was a perceptive kid, and he'd come to

know more about me than I'd realized in the 18 months we'd been working the Wheeled-meal-Robin Hood gig. I guess you can say a lot when you talk to yourself in traffic.

He brought it back up, asked me if I wanted to talk about the food poison that had traveled to my heart. I said, naw, just needed to relax and not think about what I was trying so hard to make sense of.

Billy said, "Go on, Maggie, I need a good story. You already laid the groundwork in fits and pieces. Fill in them gaps, chase them assholes away before they start building on the site."

The kid was hard to resist when he was like this and I wished he was my age so I could hold him without feeling like his mother.

This time, as the cold November sky closed in around the truck and squeezed the cab, it came out. I know my lips were moving but it sure didn't seem like I was the one telling it and there was no sign that I could've been a character in the story. I bet there are religious types that feel the same way about what they say in confession. They're certainly the ones kneeling down saying their Our Fathers and Hail Mary's, but if you tapped them on the shoulder at the alter, would they know their name or the origins of their sin?

"I'd met Derrick through a friend." I started innocently enough and turned the wipers on to smear the first few drops of rain. Yellow bug juice dripped. "Well, that friend was more of an acquaintance back then; a sworn enemy these days.

"Derrick and the enemy had been an indiscernible 'thing'," that terribly ambiguous term that could mean everything from soul mate to personal secretary to secret lover. I'd required a certain order to my life in those days, even though it was more quantum physics than calculus. I felt curiously crossed about labels. I never wanted to be a 'thing.'

"When my old friend had introduced me to Derrick at a former acquaintance's funeral, he'd been the first man to redefine the term *hope* since my divorce. Or at least put it in the same quadrant of my brain as the term 'man.'"

Billy reached for the radio and turned it off. He opened his window an inch or so and stared straight ahead, nodding his head slightly, like a dashboard doll on a smooth road. I sensed that he wasn't following my scattered intro of characters.

"There was a hitch, though, Billy." I continued.

"Always is." He turned on the defroster and unzipped his Army fatigue jacket.

"Yep," I spoke evenly as we eased onto the expressway, "A priest begins as a man. And then moves out from there into the parish, into the public world and away from what he needs, what *I* needed. It had been the tyranny of the dogma...and I was blinded by white teeth and caring eyes." I felt like I was writing a memoir instead of talking to a kid.

"I don't know what you mean by a tired dog's ma but it sounds like you hooked up with a dude that was a priest?" Billy cut to the quick of it, speaking without question in tone or assigning guilt. And for the briefest of moments, I thought he'd make a good youth minister.

"Yep," I tried to match his bluntness and plowed ahead. "But it would be over soon enough, the wine that had been water easing the beginning and the end."

Billy said to keep talking and rolled up the window. "But cut out the double meaning sentences, okay? I only go to a junior college. You sound like I'm reading a book."

I eased the big delivery truck through its eight-speed gear box and started at the beginning which was really the end. But I didn't say that.

"It was all very strange, that beautiful April morning in the big green cemetery outside Atlanta. There was a frenetic, I mean, a crazy feeling in the crisp air, more static than electric, and my forever-straight hair did a little flippy thing. But only in the back where I couldn't see it.

"Father Derrick saw it. Then looped his finders outside of his frock, touched my shoulder lightly with those long thin fingers, innocently.

'Maggie? Right?' he'd stepped away from the milling, grieving clumps of various mutuality.

"Yes, and it's Father Derrick, like the oil rig." He held my gaze, surprised at the odd, but workable name connection that moved down from my brain to the vocal chords and then out into the world as language.

"You're Stacy's friend. I met you after mass a few Sundays ago. Sad occasions, these funerals. Did you know him well? You know, the deceased?"

"You can't remember his name either?" I asked the priest.

Billy smiled and looked in my direction. I followed the broken white line. Back then my ability to analyze, de-code and then let the arrows fly had brought me a handful of painfully loyal followers, arch-enemies and legends of jealously-intrigued middle-grounders who, I thought, secretly hoped for me to be elected to some local office. Or be assassinated. "She's superbly intuitive, they'd say." But I already knew that.

Billy let out a nondescript, "Huh, so Stacy is the friend-turned-enemy," and reminded me that a green light meant you could proceed.

"I knew him, not well, but I liked him and would've made an effort to know him better." Father Derrick was dodging the question and seemed to be carrying on an important conversation with himself. "Or maybe, no, I don't remember his name because like most people, I didn't make the effort to, just relied on the fall back catechisms like *God's soldier, that crusader* and the un-corporate but up-and-comer—*Mr. Ashes to ashes*. But what's your excuse, Miss Maggie-May?"

That's how it had started, something based on the banter of the radically honest, grounded in intellect. More alpha than beta waves.

I told Billy that a lot of flesh left me that moment in the cemetery. And when Billy tapped me on the shoulder, I shuddered hard enough to push the truck into another lane.

"Whoa, Maggie, I was just reminding you to speak plainly like, so I don't have to match you with shit like, 'This guy didn't invent the rainy day for you to get wet' and such things."

I apologized to Billy, pulled my long bangs behind my ears and checked each lane, then my hair in the rear view mirror.

I composed myself and continued.

"We both worked downtown and would run into each other on the crowded, lunchtime streets, stopping and picking up conversations from two weeks prior as if we were interrupted by a phone call. Sometimes Father Derrick's assistant was there, antennae up and olfactory working overtime in search of pheromones, you know; smelling aphro…oh, never mind. Other times he was solo and my own analysis skills would scan for a difference that I'd hoped not to find.

"One night I wrote in my journal, 'eyes like a Bond-type or someone who knows something that you don't, but won't tell you unless you ask him quite specifically. Very much a quantum physical being.'

"The next week he called. Would I be interested in a newly-vacated position running the homeless shelter? It was all very much uphill from there."

Billy asked me if I was okay, if I needed to stop and get some coffee or a shot of something stonger or talk to a priest or something. I laughed and kept driving, missing all the turn-offs I was supposed to take.

"Maggie?" Billy's eyes did a separated, twisting thing—one searching for heroism, the other for fallacy.

"You ought to come clean. You ain't gonna' find a better time or place to unload your shit."

I thought to myself, what did he know that I didn't? But he was right. For a kid. And I pulled the handle of fecal memory.

"It was on a June night when I told him, the temperature inside my room rising faster than I could spin off by shedding blankets. The big moon had just hit my bay window, some kind of convection planet, I thought, inconveniently controlled by heat sources out of my control.

"The thing that held the most heat, the thing that I willed on and off, a mental thermostat, like religion, like one more drink, was a *thing* that belonged to a *who*. Father Derrick's arm seemed to be on fire; a long thick hot plate, cool to the touch but with a life force of its own burning my skin. I lifted it off my chest and set it next to his sleeping body.

"But it started as a dream, Billy. He wasn't real at first. Then, as a lover, in real life, he was unreal. More than a...father figure."

Billy stopped me for clarification. Yes, I told him. I hadn't dreamt the whole thing up. He was more than a flesh and bone figure of my imagination. Billy just nodded, like he'd heard this kind of bizarre tale before.

"Fill in the middle," Billy said, "Go back to the part where he sort of maneuvered you into a job."

I pulled the truck over into a big dirt lot next to a grocery warehouse. It began raining like the end of the world. The dirt was slick and I hoped we might get stuck. I pulled a cigarette out of the glove box. Billy said I didn't smoke but I told him I needed to do something with my hands and he said to hold his.

"I'm twice your age, kid. Don't even go there." I put a hard edge on my voice.

"Look, Maggie. I'm twenty and have worked with

you for what? Two years come March? I was raised in foster homes, lived on the streets. I seen realness, lady. If I wanted to hook up with you it woulda' happened six hours after we met."

I dropped the cigarette and rejoined the story. My hand was on his knee, under his calloused palm. If I was a mother I'd have wanted a son like him.

"Father Derrick had met me at the front gate of the 'campus,' a mid-level sprawling collection of old Quonset huts left over from '43 when FDR could procure real estate with the stroke of his seated-quill, all in the name of national defense. What remained were either bleeding heart liberal ops or $10k/square foot, Nuevo-riche, bay-view condos."

"Welcome to the land of the brave and the homes of the financially independent, Miss Maggie Mayson." Derrick the priest wore dark slacks, a standard-issue country club style polo and rubber beach slippers. He was engaging but reserved and I saw right through him. It wasn't hard and at that moment, I hated the stock I owned in foreshadow.

"Thank you, ah, Father. So…where do I start? You know, with this new job? To be honest, I don't know whether you want me to ladle soup or work up spread sheets for next month's budget."

"He took one giant step backwards, Billy, like mother-may-I, and regarded myself, his new employee, with equal parts admiration, confusion and relief. But if he was entering his own confessional he should of said, 'Bless me Father, for I'm scared shitless of how I feel about this woman.' About me."

Billy ran his fingers through his hair and said, "Oh, Jesus. You even saw the first pitch before it was thrown."

I nodded and watched the puddles in the field grow in size and depth.

"I spent the day talking to the men and women who

came to the shelter for food and warmth and a break from the beating that life was giving them. Father 'D,' as the locals called him, wasn't around. I wonder now if he wasn't spending his day in deep prayer for what he knew must be happening to him.

"We avoided each other like two playground bullies for three weeks. On the fourth Monday of my job, Father D asked me if I wanted to get a drink after work.

'You mean like, Kool-Aid from the kitchen or shall we steal some cheap wine from the refectory?' No one must've spoken to him like this. And the fear rose behind his eyes, touched the edge of his reason like a high tide. And then left with the moon."

I told Billy I was sorry but that was just the way I talked about such things and I hoped he knew what I meant. He put his arm on my shoulder and said keep it comin'. I told him how the priest reacted.

"Ah, c'mon," Father Derrick's voice searched for a kind of purchase that didn't exist. "Is it that hard for you? I'm a friend. I like you. I'm safe. And dammit, Maggie, I'm a human."

"No, you're not," I told him and his pupils encased the rest of his white space, leaving little room for reason. "You're like a Jr. Varsity God or something." And then I added, partially because I had already taken a hit from one of the old volunteer worker's hidden whiskey flasks, "You're a catch, a Valhalla, the damn forbidden fruit. So…let's go get some tequila, eh, Padre D."

"Wow." Billy rubbed the top of my hand as one might comfort the terminally ill. "Gnarly mutual hook up. Sounds to me like you were both fishing but when you found the wrong catch on the line you decided to eat it anyway."

I smiled. Billy reminded me of me.

"It lasted nearly eighteen months, Billy, and it was so outlandish that anyone who suspected felt dirty and went to say their confessions. "Bless me Father but I've had immoral thoughts, terrible images of you fucking the Head of the Homeless.

"But Father D was strong, or so he thought.

"One night, as we lay on my California Queen, the sound of a Calypso band pulsing through the floorboards, the scent of sage and Eastern incense left over from another exploratory night, I found myself in one of those places that comes on like a cold rain in August—unexpected, brilliant and cutting.

"Derrick," I rolled over on top of him, my left breast splitting the tan line that split his forearm and bicep, a place when exposed designated his willingness to bare his life and the dogma that forbade it. 'I'm pregnant. And I'm going to have it. Going to call it Derrickito. Will you do the christening?' I had become so good at this joke of cultural dubiousness that I barely recognized my own cynicism."

I stopped and picked the cigarette I'd dropped off the floorboards. Billy re-lit it for me and asked if I'd mind if he smoked a joint, said he might be able to connect culture with dubious if he was high.

"Do you ask your mother if you can get high?" I said in a nasally twinge.

I think he said, "If I only knew," but wasn't sure. The rain was making a drumming sound on the hood of the truck; loud enough to see, but not to hear. I sat in silence and remembered, saving the image for myself.

Father Derrick had searched hard for the beginnings of a smile, a twinge of the upper lip, a slight closing of the eye, an indiscernible scent that would change the polarity of every terrified molecule. And I hid them all. Let him suffer, I thought, for he knows not the pain he has caused me.

He rose from my bed and opened the seventh story window. The sounds of the city entered hard and quick, its concrete steps.

The priest vomited long and hard, all that nice

Italian food the Society had prepared in his honor only a few hours ago. Someone down below yelled up at the dark metal fire escape. The man, Derrick, responded as a steel worker might.

Billy offered me a hit and I refused, not wanting anything to dull the thick roar in my ears.

"Finish it up, Maggie. You're damn close," he said.

I was lost in that place when truth and memory run roughshod over dreams and imagination. I heard nothing but my own words as I had spoken them to my ex-lover.

"Gravity bites, don't it, Padre? I lie here soft and round and gentle for you but hard comes later, alone in that priestly-house with its volunteer-scrubbed, lemon-scented floors and pages of your next sermon fanned down on the rich, maple table.

"Were there others? Cuz, Padre D, you've spun me out in my own time—circles of seed that will grow circles of seasons where the sun won't rain and the clouds won't shine. I'm gonna' be a mommy, Father, with webs and whereabouts and that always, always wondering about his or her father. Yep, Derrick the Man, life is just a big circle that can't be squared."

Billy regarded the joint that rest between his right thumb and forefinger. It seemed to have gone out but he made no effort to relight it, just rocked his head slightly from side to side like a horse's tail trying to rid itself of flies. After a long while he mumbled under his breath something like, "Well I'll be a damn bastard," and his eyes seemed to go back in his head.

I was pulling myself together slowly, looking for the straight edges of the puzzle, moving back toward the present, lighter but not unburdened. But Billy said wait a minute.

"What about Father Derrick? I mean, what did he say?"

I looked at the kid and he appeared younger than

he had this morning. And I wondered if my baby would've grown up like him, traded from home to home like a cute but untrainable dog.

"Billy," I took the roach from his fingers and pretended to throw it out into the wet mud, "He was...amazing. After he'd lost it, he composed himself and sat on the bed, ran those long, thin fingers through my hair and spoke in a kind of trance, yep, it was an angelic trance. He spoke about children, how they squeeze their tiny fingers around yours when they're babies, how they smell so fresh and feel so pure in your arms. And he went on like that for what seemed like many days and nights but slowly something happened and he was talking about dressing them and cleaning up their rooms and picking them up from the station after they're caught stealing a Kit-Kat bar from the Piggly Wiggly. The idea of procreation seemed much different when Father Derrick stopped talking.

"He was right, Billy. I was as much at fault. I'd been the evil temptress, the forbidden fruit, somewhere between Eve, Mary Magdalene and Marilyn Monroe. I really did like the man, both as a human and a priest."

Billy fished in his pocket for another joint but didn't light it. Outside the rain had stopped and I kept talking.

"When Father Derrick had finished talking, I felt disconnected from what seemed real and what seemed too real. I wanted to post extra sentries near my heart, wanted to die but wanted to give birth too."

Billy reached over and started the truck mumbling with the unlit joint bobbling up and down between his lips.

"Let's go deliver some food," he said, "You done good but that's enough purge for today." But there wasn't much committal to his words. The bravado in his challenge to me was gone and it seemed that the fear had left my body only to find his.

I turned the keys back to the off position and rolled down the window. The air had a mixture of old and new, of clean earth and moldy air. I took the joint from his mouth, lit it and hit a long, hard pull. My lungs hurt but the pain didn't last very long.

Then I started to finish what I'd begun. Billy was staring out the passenger window. His right and left hand were holding each other as if to catch one if the other fell.

"He left that morning and said he'd call me later. But later came and I was a hundred miles down the road with $512 bucks in the pocket in my coat, one big suitcase and a fetus the size of my thumb riding shotgun. I drove until I fell asleep at the wheel and the white dots in the lane woke me up. It's funny, Billy. I wouldn't of minded driving into the ditch but I wanted to have that kid. I really did."

Billy looked at me and I couldn't tell if he loved or hated his life. The ambiguity in his eye was bouncing like a steel carom ball ready to go tilt.

"Did you dream that night?" He asked.

"What?"

"You must've had some kind of dream, some kind of woman's intuition thing going on. How did you…know?" Billy's voice rose and cracked around the edges. "How did you KNOW that he'd never try and find you?"

I took one more hit on the joint and thought that's it; I'm too old for this shit. "Yeah, I dreamt. Never forget it. And fuck you for asking, by the way." We sat there in silence for a long time and finally Billy opened his door and said he was going to hitch back to the warehouse.

"Okay, get in kid." I barley recognized the sound of my own voice. "I'll finish it."

"It was like this. There were flying fetuses in the shape of a V. They were black and white like penguins and couldn't decide to go north or south so they flew in a circle, faster and faster until they created a vortex in the air, a baby tornado and it sucked the sand up from the ground and it blinded their eyes so they starting crashing into each other and some were dying but others were laughing at how much fun they were having in this new deadly game. I heard them laughing and crying in the air, Billy, and I could smell the downy-soft feathers that seemed to be clouding in around me. But then I couldn't see any more and waved my hands at the bodies that had morphed into birds, screaming for them to stop, to leave me or behave like good little storks."

I slowed to take a breath and realized that I was crying but there were no tears on my cheeks. Billy nodded and said, "You ain't doing the last-dance-of-the-night shuffle, Maggie. Regret is different than guilt. It isn't bottomless."

I rolled down the window further and tried to spit but only air and little drops came out.

"I had that kid. I had him for three days and then the agency came and got him. All official with papers and everything. Never saw him or tried to find him. I buried him as deep as I could.

I wiped the dryness from my cheek and said that's it, that's all I have to tell. Then I started the big truck and pulled out of the muddy lot as the air got crisp with the clearing winds. We pulled onto the busy street and headed for our first delivery. I don't recall us ever being late.

Billy fiddled with the radio and watched me out of the corner of his eye. A car in front slammed on its brakes and I had to hit ours hard as well.

"Whoa, Mama," Billy had returned to his city-jargon. "We got cans of food in the back. People don't want to eat food from dented cans." We laughed a forced laugh and the normalcy tried to move back in like a returning soldier who still saw himself at war.

"Sorry, Billy-boy. I suppose I already spilt enough for the day."

Billy looked at me with those big, round, swallowing eyes of his and rolled the window down all the way, sticking his nose out like a dog.

"Nothing smells better than the truth. You know? It gets you. It just does."

"What?" I said, more demand than question. "What is truth?" I was gripping the wheel so hard my fingers had gone white.

"Truth and guilt are stony things. Sometimes they get left behind themselves or lodged in an artery like some damn rock in a creek." Billy sighed and shrunk back into the wide bench seat.

"He suffered too. He dreamt the dreams of the unbetrayed. He lived like a ghost for a long time. With chains and shit all over him."

"Who, God dammit?" I asked but already knew, the hugeness of the world shrinking me.

Billy calmly buttoned his coat as the air inside the cab suddenly went cold. "My dad wasn't an evil man. He said his penance."

I pulled the truck up to the loading dock of our first delivery wondering how, now that it was re-created, I would ever erase it again.

"You should've heard his requiem, Maggie. You can re-write the music any way you want. But you damn well better be prepared to sing. It took me sixteen less-than-sweet years to find him, Mom. And I only had him for one. But it was worth it. I don't think he was unhappy when he died."

"Let's unload this stuff," I forced what air was left in my lungs and stepped out of the cab.

We met behind the truck and the kid grabbed me by the wrist and held me close until real tears fell and mixed with the wet concrete and ran into pools that found their way into cracks that went places nobody really knows.

The white space between us could not be entered or spoken across.

It started to rain again. But the puddles shrank.

Behold, a Bright and Pale Horse

Thank you for inviting me though you have no choice in the matter. Nobody gets out of here without me.

Call me Death, for I have known every body, each requiring my stamp, my approval and my exit visa. I'm pleased to meet you, now you won't have to guess my name. Know me if you dare for the nature of me is actually quite sane.

We are neighbors, Life and I, sharing the one thing that we can—you. It isn't dichotomous at all. That's Life my friend. And me.

It's not as simple as the WWF, the Stork challenging the Grim Reaper. Black and white? Fogetaboutit. Lots of gray, friend, many hazy shades of winter. I can't expect you to grasp my existence any more than Life can be understood. I guess that Life and I share that as well, now that I think about it.

You see, even I don't fully understand me. How can you expect all those great minds and supposed critical thinkers to be able to know me? What did they believe?

Descartes? Boy did he ever get it wrong? I know a lot of people who *don't* think but therefore they still know Life. And most of them don't know me. As least Goethe knew my illusiveness. You remember, "Unrest and uncertainty are our lot."

Still, I am proud. Even as Donne tried to un-pronounce me as my name implies.

I shant die.

For if I do, you will all live with a shallow, unpalatable version of my polar twin. Too many people, not enough space, not enough food. Skinner's mice-in-the-box shit. And that whole thing with the loaves and fishes thing? It can only go so far.

C'mon, admit it, it ain't that hard to live. Life is a pretty cool chick, at least if you don't give her too much to drink. She can be an unpredictable bitch though. And as we've all seen, she makes mistakes, fucks with people's lives. But let me tell you, it's true, what they say, you know, about where some of you go after you meet me; it knows no wrath like Life scorned.

Life, as any good person, regardless of race, color and creed (BTW—I did think that quite clever. Nod to T.J.), Life gives you choices. You don't have to go and get in line to meet me. It's a dead man's party and Oingo Boingo is playing.

Like you, I have a Boss. He's the Man. Yawl have different names for Him: Yahweh, Great Spirit, The Father…He's the same cat, I tell you. We call him "G" and sometimes He's really pissed how you kill each other over what His name is. That makes a lot of work for me. But, like I said, He's the Boss so I do as He says.

When the shit really hits the fan though, I gotta' work overtime. And people blame me or Him for something that they did. You think it was me flying the Enola Gay? You think it was Him herding the Jews into the showers? Him displacing the Palestinians? It wasn't even Life after she'd gone on an all night tequila bender…it was you, you stupid little twit. From now on, when you're going to fuck up on a global scale leave me out of it. Like yo' mama done told you—use your words.

Well, at least as my friend Huxley said it when he was eyeless in Gaza, "I'm the only thing we haven't succeeded in completely vulgarizing."

Yep, go ahead and call me Death, a friend of the devil is a friend of mine and I can't wait to get home as well.

This thing in the Middle East is a damn bur under my own saddle. Geez, I guess that's why my boss put the onus on you folks. And He don't like to be used to garner votes. What a mess. Over what? Black gold? Texas tea?

You never know when someone's gonna' come

around who knows me before meeting me. Sometimes they watch my work, have born witness, have considered me, seen me, smelt me up close. My perfume is powerful indeed. I'm not hard to forget, as hard as you try. But if I can offer any advice, it is this: don't ignore me. Make my job easy. Let us meet on a quiet, windless night while you sleep in a hammock on Raiatea. Let us meet on a snowy afternoon while you nap before a roaring fire in a cabin perched beyond the clouded Continental Divide dreaming of children and children's children. Even if King Richard II called me the worst, he is true, I will have my day. It is written down in the stone, forged in the history of Man, protected by the Laws of Nature and the edict of "G."

Like Soren said, there may be fear and trembling in your sickness on your way to a job interview with me. Fear not, nor fear itself, and I will offer you the occupation of the saint, patience so that you might see the lie within the bright shining tunnel of light.

But do not romanticize nor mock me. That shit playing backwards at 78 RPM on "A Day in the Life" wasn't funny. Paul M. and I had a little chat when I picked up Linda. Be not in such a hurry, friend. I will find you. From Hamlet to Durkheim, this idea of embracing me prematurely, of jumping the metaphysical gun does not sit well with my boss the Everlasting. Look instead to the small creatures of the world, the animals, the oppressed—they survive until they are called in turn, the last first and all that. They don't charge into the jaws of Light-Brigaded Me. Look to the Natives, look to Schopenhauer because after you meet me, you will be what you were before you met me. Right, King Arthur? King Lear, King James, how about Rodney King? Didn't he ask some cool questions?

Oh, you can fight me Mr. Thomas, but if I am told to pick up a package, you can rage all you want against the dying of the light. I hath many doors. Instead, rage, rage against the other Dylan's *Masters of War*, for they have learned the trait that Woody spoke of, me as acquired taste.

They invite you to my party in which they will not attend, will not drink from the purple Kool-Aid of their own making. The men in the shadows with names like shrubs and ears like monkeys, they are mine own enemies too. Call me Death. I am on your side; if you'll let me be, speaking those Mothered words of wisdom, let it be. There is time enough, if there is time. And somewhere between the time you arrive and the time you go may lie a reason you were alive, and if in the end it is both our beginnings, before we meet, you should find out so that you know.

* * *

Call me Life, for I have known every body, each requiring my stamp, my approval, and my entry visa. I'm pleased to meet you. I see that you have met the one that comes after me, the one with the dark complexion. But Death is no threat, he and I are the same, really, just big fat bookends that try and hold this wondrously tragically hip world from spinning off its axis and into some night that even my always new boss, same as the old boss, might not go to the trouble of fetching. My job is to help you snatch the eternal out of the everlasting, to make death a way-station. I'm not religious, I just like my job.

Now, this fellow "D," who works for "G" who is more or less the same as me, we all strive toward synchronicity. And sometimes I get a bad rap because "G", he sort of lets people do their own thing and sometimes he says "game over." He doesn't have no 'splainin' to do, Lucy, 'cuz he's in the sky, with diamonds. So, I try to show people all the parts of me, wide open with possibility. I am light and dark, good and evil, happiness and tragedy; I am the laughter of a fourth margarita and the vomit on your morning floor. That's me, a light warm rain on your neck that sounds like the soft cooing of a lover unless I forget to turn off the shower and flash floods tear canyon walls from the Mother ship.

I like to think that the artists know me better than most. Sometimes they suffer for the burden of that knowledge. It smells like teen death, bleached. Oh, nevermind. Torment embraces me and I give back in ways you will only know if you have suffered the beautiful bitch that I can be. Sometimes the better ones look at me from both sides now, like Joni, from in and out and still somehow, it's my illusions I recall, I really don't know me at all.

And even though Death and I are of one mind but two worlds, we agree that we can be defined in simpler terms. We are not, as Willy S. said, "of a mingled yarn." And me, ah shucks, I'm just like a box of chocolates, the eternal text, little more than a loan shark, a dream, a disease. I am what happens, John, while yawl are busy making other plans. I am a very effective therapist, but oh as a therapist am I not ruthless? I am made of marble and mud and too short to do anything for oneself. Or is it yourself? Confused? Me too.

Somehow the Holy Trinity never turned into a metaphysical quatrain. Imagine, John the Lennon, baptized in beauty; the Father, that's G, the son, that's Jesus, the best maker of human menudo this side of Hades, the Holy Spirit, that's the unknowable, the unkillable, that's some heavy shit where the wine of life keeps oozing. But Me, I could've snuck in on the fourth hole as death did because as the Uberman said, I am too short to bore ourselves.

I am you, and you are me and we one together. There is no divide and conquer in this post-apocalyptic pretense. One half of the Fab Four, Death has met. The balance is as precarious now as in the times when I helped "G" part the Red Sea. Please do not make me measure myself out in coffee spoons. Show me, neither as it is nor as it ought to be. Call me the walrus, call me Life. For God and your own sake, keep calling. Because nobody loves me like an old man.

Or the human who is introduced to Death and panics in his presence. Embrace me. Know me and know that nobody feels any pain, just like a woman. Like Life. Like me. Keep breathing. In and out. In another world the only sure thing is that I, along with taxes, will no longer haunt your hallowed thought.

Go placidly. Strive to be happy.

Enjoy me. I am fleeting.

That Said and Undone

There's something about the way they hang under the thick mid day sun, its rays asking nutrients up from the dark blood-earth through the trunk as it sways in the trades, pumping and lifting the sugars through the branches and out toward the thick, fiery fruit. The papayas are always sweeter after the noon.

There's only one day at a time down here. And you don't have to worry about being somebody different tomorrow than you were today.

Lita would never pick papayas before the sun pasted its zenith. And even then, she will sometimes wait an extra hour or so; wait until we are just about ready to have our afternoon meal.

Then she will smile at me, her crooked white teeth a reminder of the familial past that formed the beauty that lie above and below her quiet history.

She will reach for her reed basket and tell me in her native tongue, "Voy para papaya," adding coyly, "the ones shaped like ojos de naranjo." And when I see her return with that woven basket perched atop her long black hair, dancing toward me on the trail in her blue and yellow sarong, the afternoon rain moving in on cue to cool the mid day heat as the fine, pink sand soaks up the sky like the soft part of a brain soaking up memory, one hand on the basket, the other lifting a plumeria to her nose, well...I do not think of how I got here or what I had to let go.

It's a strangely comfortable thought to look at a place and feel that maybe, just maybe, you have enough good fortune left in your life to die there; that you've earned the right to do so. But earning has little to do with anything. At least it didn't in my life.

For many years, I never figured there was any

logical sense to it, unless you count random senselessness; which, I suppose, is a kind of order in and of itself.

Some day I will think of the others, the ones that forgot too soon about what we did, what we were. They're living up on some hill with a new family to keep them out of the tragic ditches of their dreams. I won't regret not going up to see them in real time, pulling them out of a sandy pit, blood finding its way out of new holes in their bodies. That will be them, not me. Just some illogical fallacy framed around a nightmare that began as a childhood game with toy guns. They will have new lives. But old scars.

And all those months on the road I will spend, looking to make sense of what my life was and had been, just so that I could allow it to go forward. Or at least sideways. There will be no obvious order there either, just a wander, a walkabout, an unfolding and unmasking of the hope in life itself. Like Jesus in the desert. Like the desert in itself.

Maybe hope is an illusion after all; it takes you out of the eternal now. I like faith better. It lets you move between *then* and *now* without getting your feelings hurt. Think of hope as a starter kit, like when you get scared and hope you don't get shot. Then you develop the beginning of faith because even if you do catch one in the chest, you believe you have a good shot at living in another world, here inside a new skin or someplace that comes to you while laying your weapons at the alter. That's Faithville, man. And it's gotta' be solid.

It's like sawing soft wood—the blade goes through easy but you're still sawing. And you need a straight line.

It's been a few months now, but back then I could never find anything beautiful or uplifting about dying and returning to our maker. I'd heard of immortality. The third-tour guys and religious freaks torching themselves on the corner would touch upon it, but I'd never seen it in the Nam for real. And I never seen it at a funeral or in a dead body, even when I went looking for it.

What I learned about dying, I learned through staying alive, by accident not design, by letting myself get too close to the ones that left me. That died. Death on its own taught me nothing. But the process of life bubbles right to the surface when you know that yours or one who you've gotten to know, even like, that their time is close. Holding your hands inside a buddy's gut ripped open by a frag grenade, pinching off a spurting artery and talking to him just like you were speaking over the backyard fence with your garden hose bent in half to stop the water while you chatted about the game or the new boat he was looking at and lying to him that it was just a flesh wound, that he'd be getting a month in Tokyo for recovery, that lucky son of a bitch, and about this one place that you knew of where the girls were soft and went down as smooth as the sake, and to hang in there, "cuz it was nothing the docs couldn't fix," and medics were on the way and they'll give him some morphine and he'd feel better, now close your eyes and get some rest but before you do look at me, now look at me god dammit, don't you fucking go and die on my ass 'cuz we got stuff to do back in the world. Now, look in my eyes…you hear me, mother fucker?

You owe me!

You keep lying to him until the soft sounds of heart's footsteps don't echo in sync with the thump-thump of the Hueys and he won't keep his eyes open and your criteria for falsity and truth is further cultivated by the schizophrenia you embrace like a three-year-old fondling a dead sparrow.

You'll be all right, and then you hold him like you held your mamma when you got lost in the big store. And he holds you back and whispers words unnamed and unknowable.

Then the son of a bitch is dead gone and for a brief moment you forget his name but remember his kid's birthdates and the color he planned on painting his Chevy

Camaro when he got back.

You go on living, knowing more about life because when he looked into you with those young, scared eyes, he passed all that he knew and felt and had learnt in-country along as a kind of gift that would open on its own accord, on its own time, anyplace but there.

All this he did for you, partly because he could, partly because you would've done the same. All this happened right before that long, deep sigh.

And if per chance, he screamed and called out in some language of the lost or at least the losing that you couldn't respond to, you've had to chase that sound away with every ghost that came back and you purposely, palpably, exorcised them all on the outskirts of towns like Nogales or Santa Fe or Laramie or Durango. Like a rabid dog, you could either shoot them dead or shoo them into the next town. But no more guns please. And so you bargained and closed your eyes and hoped for the best. Never sure. Cognitive Dissonance, the docs at the VA called it. And you lived with it like a forever rash until one day that three-year-old girl opened her hand to offer you the dead sparrow only it was a yellow and white daisy. And a map to the Promised Land of DMZ's.

Things are good here, though. What happens from day to day still can't be called order so much as rhythm; a natural ebb and flow, a simple existence with Lita, our daughter, Makoi, the local villagers and our immediate world on this island off the coast of South America. An archipelago for the wounded of soul, Father Damien could come step off the copra supply boat with a handful of faceless and fingerless and nothing would matter. War is just a different kind of flesh-eating disease.

An island. Ironic, but not really. I would've thought I'd end up in a more stable spot, geographically-speaking, assuming I didn't end up under the ground. Most of the islands in this region are old though, they aren't fluid and moving and spewing new earth out of their highest peaks. But they haven't been aged at the hands of modern man either. This is young adult land—old enough to have an idea of where it's going but not grown cynical from the journey. I thought about the island's teen years, when fiery molten worlds moved villages and added to the shores, leaving a steaming mist as it mixed with the sea and the sulfur hung in the air for weeks, sighing. But things down here don't follow chronological time. People grow sideways before growing up.

The fluid earth; that must've happened a long time ago. But even then, people were fighting over something—land or religion or politics or women. The earth must've been a violent place to live during those six days when God was the GC or the sixty million years it took for the world to evolve organically. Either way, there are days I'd argue that it got worse as soon as man came around.

Before I leave the Nam I'm gonna' go and talk to one of the guys from the 31st Airborne, tell him I'm going off the grid, going south. Flyboys have a different perspective. He'll probably say once you come back from the Nam, don't matter what you do with your life 'cuz they ain't never gonna' let you back on. Not completely. He'll say I wasn't the only one been opening doors on themselves; tell me to go forget about quadrants and little squares with borders that you only know about when you pass a sign or a checkpoint. He'll say the great blue world scattered with green dots; that's more like the beginning of it all. Personally, he'll say, there's places most guys ain't looked under their pillow.

I'll respect him for that but agree that I'd likely be happier in a place with no certifiable history of the kind that I was used to; the kind that had sent us to do unconscionable things for their premeditated good.

Fighting for your sanity is a different war all

together; a sustained, protracted jungle warfare that somehow seems at place within the vines and branched-synapses of your brain. But it's not like you can go to safety behind your own lines for R and R. You don't even carry it. It carries you. There's *no peace with honor* bullshit. Only a form of mutual détente.

I will conclude that it was all irrevocably pre-determined. Maybe not genuine in my reflection of the moment, but truthful in the end because at some point, and I don't know exactly when, I stopped looking for answers in my past and decided to let them find me in the present. I stopped fighting and was given the medal of *Who-Gives-a-Fuck.* Let the devil's germs and guns and concerns move in the front door and out the back. More Buddha, less Beowulf.

Those ideas live in me now, like an ageless lap dog, forever loyal and available. Life down here is one long poem where I can bring up the ghosts one at a time and write them a shape, shake hands and then wait for the trades to blow them away.

They still visit but they don't stay.

Life, if we cut it up, it dies in the process, killing those around us too, plain as day. Killing taught me that. Not fluffy bunny rabbit moments.

Yet some nights when I lie in our hammock and the sweat comes beading little islands of salt on my body-map, I'm injected by the jungle sounds and smells, and am tripped to '68 and Hueys and Tet and Sweet Jane and inventing separate realities when I needed them and an enemy wearing pajamas that played prairie dog with the rest of us who are walking around in the sun and the rain stuck halfway between Kumbayaa and Eve of Destruction. Simple grunts. Superior technology, my ass. Kids from poor cities trying to find a way up through the choking seaweed of urban streets and domino-theory McCarthyism; we'd have been better off in black pajamas and a real reason to kill.

But then I close my eyes, weave my arms and legs through Lita like all those vines of my past and let my mind take me where it will. As I fall asleep or go a few rounds with Morpheus, our hearts flow together like water until I can't tell where I end and she begins and the last sound I hear is her own humming and my submission to the white noise of the world. It's the sound of a long deep sigh.

Fear turns men into coyotes, poisons their hearts. I guess that whoever lit my flame certainly has the right to blow it out. Way down there, I won't be afraid of the pain. When its gets too heavy to lift, brush aside or takes on a new disguise, I can burrow my lined and leathered face deeper into Lita's brown-skinned breasts, her innocence acting like some sort of filter, some South Pacific dream catcher that takes the hurt and softens it or gives meaning to the nightmare stepping on it.

Yep, closer I get to tomorrow, the further I get from today.

* * *

I've come to believe that the best stories always begin at the end. They begin with a dream. Dreaming this way always helps to thaw the sea that has frozen around my heart. I believe its truth and its lies as much as the lies of the Nam that try to swallow me now, here in Danang, only 40 days and a wake up from a bird back to the World that may not know me ever again. The blood of amnesia is on its hands.

One day I will emerge unvanquished. Forty days and a wake up.

And someday I'll get my island and my Lita, my manifest turned destiny that right now, banks want to foreclose on before papers are drawn and quartered. Someday, I won't be afraid of the dark.

I will learn how to cry again.

Only forty days and a thousand nights from my

grid-less land of papayas and no telling one day from the next. I can pull a straight forty. I am Jesus in the desert.

Tempt me. Go ahead.

This is where I begin. I can feel it now in the words scribbled on the back of a desert menu from the Continental Hotel in Saigon.

War, I've done. The rest will jump off the screen in Technicolor; brilliant, edible and equally dangerous.

Real

In Search of the Last Hippy, Approximately

"If you want to live outside the law,
you have to be honest."
Bob Dylan

Everything in here, but the sum of its parts, is real. Some of it even approaches the truth of my tongue. I was going to the funeral for a friend. But I was going hunting as well.

I was going in search of the last hippy, clinging to a long patient ideal, a vibrating notion that sent me in search of hair. I wouldn't call it a mid-life crisis exactly, but my pre-Aquarius dating was haunting me. I needed to find a flower child, receive the holy sacrament of hash, if not the free love of copulatory communion. I needed to find the last hippy, approximately.

Tin Soldiers and Nixon had come and gone only to be replaced by the Executive Branch of United Chevron Nations. Pharmaceutical agents, yoga, tofu and Taro Cards had all failed me. I had to go back to the few things I remembered in the mirror—May of '68 and an incense burning, pubescent punk with an older sister.

I had gone back because when I was about to be called up, I went completely sideways.

I traveled north to U.C. Berkley where there had been reports of sightings, Bigfoot in beads, day-glow posters on creosote poles, acoustic guitars slung low and slouching toward the Bethlehem of free speech. And that sweet smoke wafting west to where the sun fought the horizon.

At the information center, a ghost-colored student with thick-bottled lenses rose from a thicker bio-text and studied me with nasally disdain.

"Hippies? Try the Discovery Channel or get-a-life.com."

There had to be one Leftist still breathing in this former bastion of political activism; just one young American who'd stand up, or sit down for what's right, or at least one '63 VW Bus driving further, further into the past. I prayed for the simple possibility.

Wandering the vast rolling beauty of the campus in search of anyone not welded to a walkman or cellular device, the students looked so young, so studious, so...entrepreneurial. The old stone buildings had alumni donor names freshly carved into the ancient stone façade. A small, study group of aloof Asian kids spoke quietly among themselves. It was that sing-song diction of cyber-speak, the language of six-figure starting salaries. The scattered art on the grounds that I remembered as "engaging" now looked rusted and industrial-safe. And among the spring-green redwoods, now tired and thick, their weighted branches held aloft with guy-wires and keep-off signs, stood newer concrete structures, re-bar gray and Molotov-proof. Where were the red slashes and yellow bandanas?

I followed the smell of fresh beans past the Hearst Library and the Zellerbach Business School toward a clean well-lighted place with the words *Free Speech Café* routed into a piece of thinly varnished plywood. The walls were papered in black and white murals of bright faces; Mario Savio with a bull horn looking angry, concerned, speaking freely. Savio had died in '96 from heart troubles. He was fifty-three, dead before he got old, electrically charged before his own somatic institution shut him down.

I read the caption and closed my eyes to hear the words:

"There is a time when the operation of the machine becomes so odious, makes you so sick at heart, that you can't take part; you can't even passively take part, and

you've got to put your bodies upon the gears and upon the wheels, upon the levers, upon all the apparatus, and you've got to make it stop."

The only wheels and gears I'd put my body on when Savio delivered those words in '64 were attached to the chain on my little bicycle. The machines had changed but people were still chained to them, not knowing what for.

I took my three-dollar coffee and tried to drag a patio chair into the sun but it was bolted to the concrete floor and I swore under my breath. What was I here for? Oh, that's right, another eulogy, another death at 53, another good heart gone bad. It was my turn to speak in front of the Berkeley Brass about an injustice, albeit a singular one. My young friend with the old heart, Brian Maxwell, was dead. Brian had run 2:14 for the marathon, had been on the Canadian Olympic team. Nothing wrong with his ticker.

Wrong.

He'd left a wife and six young kids in his wake, wondering. The good they die young.

I had expected to find inspiration in the past, all which came to me was a point of intersection where memory played leap frog between then and now and the present became its own dimension. It was the tyranny of the urgent. Instead, I felt sick. Was there no one left who would rage against the death and dying of the tie-dyed ethos? Was it all a diethylamide dream woken by narcan and dwindling numbers; that eve of destruction gone quietly into the dying light? Who killed Davey Jones and my friend Brian Maxwell? What hammer stopped his young and wild heart?

I marched down Telegraph Ave. past Rusputin's Records where you could once buy rolling papers that sold for a nickel, past Shakespeare and Co. where you could get a copy of *On the Road* for a buck, past the neuvo-vendors hawking bangles that dangled from piercings an evenly increasing number. And then up to People's Park where I imagined a crowd had taken in with me a dozen strong. But then only to realize after arriving that they'd all lit out for the bin of free clothes and pawed through the big plywood box for anything they could take and sell.

Somehow I sensed that I might be closer. Something in the depravity gassed my cynicism and I knew the last hippy, approximately, would be here.

I scanned the bulletin board and saw an ad to make $15 an hour from your home, no plasma required. I watched a couple kiss and heard one of them complain about his lover's scratchy beard. I saw a basketball game of smack-talk and chain nets below the bent rim, but no ball. I saw people sleeping in red sawdust, spooning their lives in needles of pine and steel. I saw prom queens lost to hard time and soup lines and the bitterness of faded rouge. I saw shoeless, fatherless, fearless children on soundless swings, the bearings long since gone, and the polished metal bushings smooth and efficient.

I felt the future but it came up cold and hard-edged against the hope of what had passed.

But there, off in the mimsy borogorves of a few pale maples stood a middle-aged man with a garden hose, real water flowing onto a young garden. He wore the tapestry of kings, a proud bed-sheet robe. And he spoke freely, concern in his intentioned eyes, his lips offering some inane immutable truth to no one save the white rabbit in his mind.

I approached him from behind and asked if he was the last, approximately. He turned slowly, not noticing that he had watered the ground below my feet.

"Tell Jann he promised me the cover," he said. "We had a deal." And then he moved back inside his garden and his pulpit.

To think about resistance is to think about acceptance. Not for sale or selling out. Everything is true and nothing is true. And quantum physics never did get you that four-bedroom, three-bath in the burbs. War is hell but heaven has left earth, left the building with Elvis. What we have now is an Ipod zeitgeist, Rollerball come true, Vacuum Ville. Everything is gone but the uncertainty of some goodness. Free love replaced with free downloads, nothing but rising temps and falling forests, endangered species replaced by pocket-pets. I don't want to live in an air-conditioned world and I'll never learn to speak Chinese. I'd gone to a friend's funeral but a lot more had passed.

And these kids, the students of Bezerkley, don't they care? Okay, previous generations didn't leave things in such great shape. But who ever really cleans a hotel room? I ain't buying that "I'm only a dot in a dot.com world" shit. It's just work, baby...just connecting the political with the personal, as someone said.

Walking back up the avenue, I was compelled to revolt at the repulsion, disgusted that I was still unable to distinguish the peace agents from the sales agent, unable to speak out against the slick genocide with a Jeffersonian air and plane old Grace. The best I could do was to jaywalk into a Starbucks and take a piss without buying anything at all.

I miss the obvious ambiguity of the war.

Someday I'll go there on vacation for the first time.

Yeah, me and the ghost of Hanoi Jane. Stepping over the land minds of our past.

Crooked Timber

"This face is all I have, worn and lived in;
the lines around my eyes my old friends."
Willie Nelson

I asked the nurse if she ever got used to the smell of burning flesh. She looked away from me and spoke through the white surgical mask, the same kind I had used to paint the bathroom the weekend before.

"Sure, you just don't notice it after awhile."

Notice *what*, I thought, the smell, or the act of burning someone's flesh itself?

She must have sensed my confusion because she forced an awkward laugh, covering some deeper thought by making light of a serious situation. I'm sure she knew I was hiding behind a thin layer of macho veneer; this stable women who cauterized each small blood vessel as the surgeon sliced away another layer of my face. She knew, they always do. It's their job.

My job was to be "okay" with the operation the docs were about to perform. Regardless of the outcome, whether a tiny snaking scar or Elephant Man, I needed to be ready.

I wasn't.

Cynicism is a bad thing. And I was cynical about plastic surgery, a term that isn't as apparent or descriptive as its semantic partners, "reconstructive" and "cosmetic." Vain men and women standing in line, I thought, paying huge sums of money for what is known as elective surgery (you choose to have it—there is no real medical need). Flip through the pages in the office, order off the menu. You want pouty lips, smooth cheeks, a thinner waist, thicker calves, high-beam boobs? The before/after pictures are always convincing.

But I'm a guy. Men can get away with crows feet around the eyes and a few jagged lines left over from a motorcycle crash or an old football injury. Women *need* to look half their age. It says so right there on the cover of *Redbook*, *Cosmo* and *Women's Day*. Forty-year-old guys who model underwear are considered rugged and must've been a famous jock at one time or another. Forty-year-old women do ads for estrogen supplementation.

Yeah, I was a real righteous cat. I may have appreciated the outline, if not the sculpture of augmented breasts (you really can't say "fake tits" anymore), but when I felt them, I was taken back to my days on the beach, shoveling jelly fish into plastic bags to clear the volleyball court. (I can hear the collective sneer of men everywhere.)

The job I was in for wasn't elective though. Unless you count the result of a chosen lifestyle. I was getting cut on because things had spread. Bad cells doing bad things.

It's funny. There I was, lying there under the beady lights, waiting for some lab technician with thick glasses and bad teeth to come back and tell the doc if things were cool. It's the sins of my youth that had placed me in this predicament, the endless summer days out in the water, surfing, swimming, just plain hanging with my buds on the hot sand. The messenger lab rat had pasty white skin, no wrinkles. Probably served a volley ball under hand. I bet he hadn't been laid in months.

Punk couldn't *earn* the bitch named skin cancer. And I was jealous. This wasn't by-choice surgery. My choice had been to play outside in the sun, all my life, mostly without a hat. Now, *this* was my price, no-free-lunch and all that. It wouldn't kill me but I could end up looking, well…cut and pasted, bio-photoshopped.

Somewhere in the take-the-patient's-mind-off-the-procedure conversation, sunscreen entered the dialogue.

Oh, you mean that white stuff that the lifeguards put on their nose, like a seagull shit on their beak? Naw. Sunglasses are fine.

We were kids, immortal. We were surfers.

Technically, it wasn't my face under deconstruction, but my nose, which sits on top of the face. I knew that it was commonly felt by most surgeons that a nose is much more difficult to rebuild when sliced and diced away; more difficult than, say, a shoulder or a thigh. With a bad hair style, you can always hide an ear. Noses are tough.

Right down the hall, in the lobby of my next stop after the dermatologist had finished with this "office visit," were half a dozen women thumbing through the pictorials that would shape their future by shaping their flesh. Most of them would be waiting to have the plastic surgeon alter their physical appearance in some way; almost always in an effort to look younger. Nobody goes to a plastic surgeon wanting a more mature look.

I was running from what'd happened in my youth. They were struggling to hold onto theirs.

And as the dermatologist came back in to take "just one more small section" from my left temple ("Let's just snag this little beauty as long as we have you here"), another basal cell carcinoma, ("Oh, nobody dies from these"), the nurse with the soldering gun in tow stood ready, like a gunnery sergeant feeding a string of 50 caliber bullets into a machine gun. She was ready to stop the bleeding by welding the ends of those little bleeders shut.

Why would anyone *choose* to have their body cut into, onto, moving flesh around like clay on a potter's wheel? Why would you make a conscious decision to have someone cut you open? Why not run a few more miles, pad your bra, and put that white crap on your nose? But we know why, I think, the reasons lying inside our subconscious, sandwiched between repressed pain and thrilling anticipation.

The shape of a person's body, especially the face, is

the windsock for the rest of their being. We are subtly taught this through our means of socialization, from the school principal's disciplinary scowl, to watching our mothers apply their make-up before leaving the house, to the deodorant commercials that feature former *Baywatch* types. A chiseled jaw, man or woman, is external evidence of internal strength and resilience. A furled brow means intensity, worry, sometimes anger. And the eyes, the so-called windows to the soul, they speak volumes that we are unable to hear. If a skilled surgeon can give us what was not a standard feature at birth, tighten up what age, gravity, kids, stress and sun have lowered, then why not, the entitled will ask?

"Raises the self-esteem," we are told, "puts back what should be there." The anecdotes are fast, furious and compelling. Most women who opt for elective surgery state that they need to feel more beautiful for themselves, not those who look at them. More out of compassion for the concept than true understanding, I can almost embrace those claims.

"I love my kids," a woman will say, "but they ruined my boobs."

If I was a woman, listening for 20 years to every other man turn to his friends and say, "Bro, check out that rack," I'd could probably convince myself that a great rack would open a few doors.

Men, face it—it's our own damn fault.

It must be hard to fight that particular stereotype, all that white noise telling women how important mammary glands are. Our society says they should be firm, shapely, and if possible, large. That is *our* society though, an important footnote.

Usually, when a small skin cancer, lesion or mole is removed, the kindly nurses pull down their masks to let you see their sincerity and say its all fine, the doc will just put a few stitches in the area to keep it shut tight and clean while it heals up and disappears into a small inconvenience of the past.

When the last biopsy report finally came back with "clear margins," I heard none of these benign pleasantries, only, "Well, the plastic surgeon doing the closing is very good." Nurses are healers, they have access to the drift of things to come, whether appealing or appalling.

Dog eat dog, I thought, sun eat skin, skin eat flesh, cut or be killed. No love at all in looking good early, then flaming out.

I tried to comfort myself with the snippet of knowledge that Robert Redford refuses to have a face lift against the constant request of movie studio heads.

I knew this was more than a "closing." The removal of the epidermis and dermis layers off my nose had crossed this inconvenience over into the realm of reconstructive surgery, the same type used when someone puts their head through a windshield. Again, my research had told me that noses were the trickiest to get right, whatever that means. You just don't slice off a little piece from your ass or behind your ear and stick in on like play dough. There are things to consider—like blood supply and airways. Aesthetics are nice, but first you have to make sure the flesh and skin you relocate will take to its new location. Ever move a beautiful healthy rose bush to another part of the yard and come back from vacation to find the sucker dead?

In certain indigenous cultures, an elder is given great respect for having earned the deep crevices running down his or her face like vertical rain gutters. Old black and white photos of the great Native American Chiefs show unforgettable features that command respect and knowledge with a knowing sense of grace and compassion. Other tribes around the world will alter their appearance, mostly by piercing and tattoos, to make themselves more desirable to the opposite sex or to display physical prowess.

Walking around college campuses these days, I can't say that the piercing/tattoo thing is much different from Zulu culture or New Hebridian fashion of the 1800's.

The great Apache warrior Geronimo said, "I will fight no more forever."

I promised myself that I would use more sunscreen. Forever.

Interestingly, in the upcoming years disease may finally affect fashion. What some experts are saying is that due to the rapid advancement of skin cancers, within a generation, two at the most, tan skin will no longer be equated with the outdoor leisure class—the athletic types who ski, golf and ride mountain bikes instead of working real jobs. One has to wonder if at some point our society would return to the pugmarks of a century ago, when pale white skin meant that the individual didn't have to work. They could sit on the veranda all day and sip ice tea. Watching my fifteen-year-old daughter refuse anything higher than sunscreen number seven, I have my reservations.

The cultural ideology of youth-centrism is pervasive, a billion dollar industry. The myth of immortality has become its own political economy. Kids who've never heard of *The Who* don't necessarily want to die before they get old. But they might consider death before *looking* older.

But what is age anyway? A numerical designation of one human's existence. The tennis icon, Andre Agassi makes the finals of the 2005 U.S. Open at 34 years old. The NY Times labels him, "the geezer of the finals." And arguably, the greatest baseball pitcher of all time, Satchel Paige, who played his last professional game in 1965 at fifty-nine years old, once asked, "How old would you be if you didn't know how old you were?"

I thought I was too young for anything resembling a medical "operation." Too much association with bad stuff. With things that old people need.

Preparing for surgery is an interesting ordeal, sort of a micro version of being inducted into the army. They make sure that you are, in fact, who you say you are, take away your clothes and hand you a generic gown—no different than army fatigues or prison blues. You remove all of your jewelry, even the little cross that you had worn around your neck since 6th grade. It's all very humiliating, this deconstruction of one's pride.

And so many forms to sign. Yes, *I* would be the responsible party and pay the bill if my insurance company, whom *I* responsibly paid every month, failed to do so. Yes, *I* would hold harmless all the doctors and nurses who would be working on me. Hey, it's not their fault I was raised a beach rat.

You lie there on the stainless steel table, lights so bright they seem as if they could worsen your skin cancer just from lying under them. And all sorts of things run through your mind. You are giving up control to a man or a woman who is just like you, but went to school a few more years, men and women who you can't see behind the masks. I would have liked to see a powerfully cut jaw under the sterile garb, not a furled brow behind the glasses. This masked person will decide how you look. The surgeons play God with your flesh. And you breathe the gas that gives them the permission.

In the waiting room I had flipped through the generic pamphlets from the American Society of Plastic Surgeons. The one touting forehead lift read, "You'll be very pleased with your refreshed and rejuvenated appearance." Another one on liposuction stated that, "you may notice that clothes fit more comfortably and you'll feel more confident about your appearance." I wondered if teenagers got much of their confidence from the current trend of baggy clothes. Old men walk my neighborhood and their pants sag in the rear just the same. A cultural bridge, I thought, and wondered if I would mention that to my teenage son.

Oddly, as the minutes ticked away, I was becoming okay with all this. I kept hearing the quote from Dr. Beck Wethers, a member of the ill-fated Everest exhibition where more than a half dozen people died. He had been given up for dead, lost in a blinding snow storm at 28,000 feet but somehow managed to survive a night outside of the protection of the tents. In the morning he stumbled, mummy-like, into the morbid camp, most of his extremities already decomposing with frostbite.

Months later, not enough fingers and toes left to count "this-little-piggy" on, he very calmly looked at his interviewer who was wondering, then asking, "What does it feel like?"

It's only body parts, Wethers told him, only body parts.

I knew what had to be done. The plastic surgeon, a likeable craftsman with a top-shelf reputation, had shown me a digital picture of my face, sans nose and a good chunk of the left temple; just walked right into the room, opened the file, looked at the photo, showed it to me and said, yep, we have some work to do. That honesty was comforting. I like no-bullshit people, especially no-bullshit docs. I could see hanging out with this guy, loaning him tools, trusting his golf score. He seemed the right age: old enough to have some experience but not burnt out on his job.

I signed forms, thought about women getting fake boobs for Christmas, put on my backless gown and flashed on kids born with cleft pallets. Climbing up onto the operating room table, I suddenly realized how body parts have become action verbs.

"Get a leg up on that project," "Don't try to strong arm him," "Face the music pal; you just have to stomach it," "have the heart to finger your way through the problem." Beck Wethers' body parts had become part of the vernacular of success, some type of urban legend lexicon.

Suddenly, I was connected to every human being who had been operated on, who had gone under general anesthesia, who had slept the sleep of the chemically-induced necessity.

I was egoless because I had no choice. Forced Zen was better than none at all.

And that moment I realized that wounds resonate in some shared experience. That violation of external integrity creates an internal bond for all those who are affected. But they must accept it. If I was to look like the elephant man, I would need some training.

I was reminded of a friend who died twice so that he could live once—the first time when hit by a bus resulting in the loss of a leg, and again when he was struck by a truck causing his paralysis from the chest down.

"Oedipus," he would always say, "was haunted by a wound for which he had no basis of fear. And a denial of one's wound is like a denial of one's life." Where does strength like this come from? The body is only a carrier he would tell me in moments of quiet reflection. What was I carrying around inside me that needed anything but a hole in my face that let air in and air out? The importance of shape began to lose its import.

A precise moment finds a precise feeling. But the whole paradigm was still a bit cloudy. In my internal struggle I was hoping for a precision job, while losing my disdain for elective surgery, remembering all the while that the surgeon had told me, "the cosmetic funds the reconstructive."

Hey, people are lucky to have choices. They want liposuction? Fine. Go for it. If I opt to run 60 miles a week, eat less and look at silicone boobs in a whole new light, well, that's not hard either.

Yes sir, choices are good.

Something heroic was colliding with a real life reality TV show. Against all odds, maybe I was growing up—maturity moving in like a metaphor. The far-reaching fun, the sun, the sins, the unparalleled joy tailored in behind me, in sync. Just so long as I didn't make any sudden moves under the knife.

This augmentation of my own had given me this unique relationship to every woman with after-market breasts (though not in the way most men would have liked). It would connect me to every cosmetic surgery ever performed, no matter the reason or rationale behind it. Our complimentary wounds did not come at the hand of fate behind the bumper of a truck; they were lifestyle-catalyzed, one backward, one forward.

I asked my surgeon if he would rather stick to the more altruistic side of his chosen profession, just focus on the necessary things like mugs torn up in car crashes and noses lost to the Endless Summer.

"Sure," he replied, "but then I'd be driving an old car like yours."

And who was I to judge? My wife used to have great boobs. Now we have two great kids. It was a good trade. She will never go silicone; it's not in her nature. I could probably come to like a pair of those firm, perky bolt-ons, but the novelty would wear off like a new pair of sunglasses that scratch.

There are those who say that the human body is only a vehicle for the soul. You can believe that or not. But there is no denying that it will decompose at some point. The Egyptians worked really hard to slow that process. And the Indiana Jones types had a field day peeling off the layers. Still, those people had indeed checked out a long time ago, with or without souls.

Like everybody, I don't want to live out my sunset years battling some chronic disease. I don't smoke; eat healthy, drink only in moderation and exercise more than regularly. The stress is kept in check and other than a few aches and pains from time to time, I seem to be moving through the mid way mark better than most.

Okay, the sun is turning my face into the cracked dashboard of a '67 Buick Skylark left in a Phoenix back yard. But with a bag over my head or a 10k race to run, I can pass for half my age. Considering my active past, I would rather be run over by a Marlboro truck, that large picture of a rugged cowboy staring down on me from the side flashing my last view on earth, than struggling with the Big C or chronic pulmonary disease for the last five or ten years of life. It's not so much the fear of pain, but more the inconvenience of it all. I would feel like I failed, like I should have gone out the way I lived, in a fiery ball; better to, as Neil Young said, *burn out than fade away.*

Physical reification is not a course taught in grad school and we cannot touch the brakes of our lives the same way we touch the dreams in our heads.

I told the doc I just wanted a local anesthesia. He laughed and said no I didn't. How about a half way thing, like they do when they pull out wisdom teeth? That would be my choice but he would be doing some intricate work around my face—ship-in-a-bottle stuff. If I became irritable, itchy, and squirmy or pissed off, I could screw up his concentration and then they'd knock me out anyway.

Shit, I thought, then knock my ass out. But I'm not staying over night. And when can I get back in the water? There was a good south swell due to hit.

Talk to me Beck Wethers. Hey doc, measure twice, cut once.

"Kid," he said, "You cannot be simultaneously dispassionate, dry, emotionless, imperturbable, indifferent, indurated, inexcitable, passionless, phlegmatic, placid, poker-faced, reserved, reticent, self-contained, stoic, stolid, taciturn, unconcerned, unemotional, unexcitable, unfeeling, unflappable and god damn concerned about how your frickin' face will look after I pour my heart and twenty years of skill into it." And as I looked up into the cool, steely blue eyes of the anesthesiologist, I nodded, said he was slowly melding conversation with conversion and counted backwards from 10 to 9 to 8 to…

When I woke up in post op, I felt as if I had been on a three-day tequila bender in Tijuana—bent, spun, oozing from new found holes in my body, bleeding pale memories of where I was, who I had been with? Did I choose this? Earn it? Or deserve it? Trying to talk, the words slithering out of my mouth at a fresh faced nurse, no mask covering her kind words… well?

"It went great. You'll be happy." Cool. Chicks dig…oh, never mind. Where's my shorts and t-shirt? No offense, but I'd kindly like to get the fuck out of here. This place makes me nervous.

I have a nose again, and a degree of bilateral appearance between the sides of my temples. They're not pretty, but I never was. I won't be doing underwear commercials, but the nose works. Air goes in, air comes out. Even that Marlboro Man is air-brushed rugged on purpose.

And my wound makes me unique, connected.

James Hillman (Suicide and the Soul, 1965) suggests to us that the place where we are most vulnerable must be most venerated, "for they mark a sacred place in us that we would have ignored."

A broken heart over a failed love affair comes to mind. But so does that white shit that lifeguards wear on their nose.

The flesh moved deftly by my-new-best-friend the surgeon, from one side of my nose to the tip, seems to be holding up so far. The scars will improve with time, fading to a feint reminder of some false sense of youthful immortality. More skin cancers will appear and I will deal with them as I must. Sadly, hundreds of thousand are walking around in the same position.

My enlightened friend in a wheelchair says I look like an Irish alcoholic that was in a bar room knife fight—an image that is not too far from where I could've ended up. I just got there early.

And artificially.

I realize that Kant was right. If I am but a member of humanity, no perfectly straight thing will ever be made of this crooked, sun-burnt timber.

I've made my peace with silicone.

Life Be Proud

"And if you gaze for long into an abyss,
the abyss gazes also into you."
Frederick Nietzsche

I'm just driving around digging holes in every dry creek bed and big, open field that I come across. It's past midnight and in the back of my truck are two shovels, a pair of gloves and a large green tarp. I'm digging holes because it's the only thing I can think of doing right now. I need a grave but truth be known, the feel of shovel into earth is primal—I need to punish myself as well.

My twelve-year-old son sits next to me, steady as a battle-worn veteran. "It's not your fault dad. The poison was way up high in some neighbor's wood pile. Someone must've knocked it down." He's right, I try to convince myself, but I have to feel the pain of remorse, wallow in the guilt until some sad wisdom of compromise finally gains a rational foot hold. I won't dig potential graves all night long, but I might hemorrhage in other ways for months to come.

It took me thirty years to find the perfect dog: gentle with a strong spirit, inquisitive but compliant, friendly yet protective, as loyal as a bark to tree. And now she lie inside a green tarp in the back of my truck, her lithe and limber six-year-old legs stiffening with each new hole I dig, deeper and wider to accommodate, in sync with the daggered-reality that come the next morning, I'd call out her name in the pre-dawn chill to go run...and then I'd remember.

"Dad, maybe we'd just better take her home and call some place in the morning that does this kinda' stuff."

"No, we can bury her right. That's the least I can do

for…," then I'd wipe my dirty sweat shirt across my eyes and fish the back roads of my brain for the smallest reconciliation of peace.

I'd been sitting in a chair when I heard the news from my wife, "I think something is seriously wrong with Molly," she pushed the air out of her chest and into the phone. "I think she might be even…dead."

Everything went out from underneath me—the chair, my office floor, the earth. And then there was no real estate left for me to put her memory into.

I'm not a pure animal lover. That makes it worse, because when you find one you like, you latch on to it to prove to yourself that you aren't a callous asshole. The dog knows that and all the while you think you're training them, they're teaching you. Dogs know more than we ever give them credit for. Molly knew she was dying a full day before she laid down on the back deck in the sun, careful to lay her head facing away from the house so that the kids wouldn't have to see her before my wife came home and covered her up.

The morning she died, she had the saddest look of any living creature I'd ever seen. Her eyes were trying to capture us, pull us inside of her so that we could see the damage and pain of the poison; the way it must've been eating her alive, one organ at a time. It was a soundless scream for help, "I'd love to go running with you, dad , but I'm dying and it hurts like hell. You go ahead." And as always, I was late for something; just waved through the window as my wife ran her hand through her fur a few times and checked on her uneaten food while I left them—one to come back to and cry with, the other forever.

There were other signs that were missed; the way she walked a dead man's walk, head down, eyes seeking purchase on anybody who could help, tail flat and somber.

I didn't arrange her birth; didn't even raise her from a pup. She was a "pound dog," the best kind. Some other jerk missed the wholeness in her spirit while complaining that she couldn't point or that she'd dug holes in his putting green lawn. I brought her home and we became kin. We respected each other.

"Hey mom," the kids might've said, "Molly looks sick." She might've barked, or growled or thrown up blood or lie down in the middle of the room and refused to move. A lot of things might've happened. I might've thought better about even knowing that rat poison lived on my street. Death…not if, but when? Would of, should of…shit. Life is a choice, I thought, not hastily. Death isn't.

But in a gallant and gracious death as this, when one of God's creatures cannot heal themselves and then go off into the forest to die alone rather than bother the clan, they are mythologized in the hearts of those who might've done something. In cultural history passed down through oral tradition, campfire tales and classroom textbooks, they become legend. The Hero's Journey cannot belong only to the world of men.

Thirty years and I had the perfect dog in the back of my truck, cold and stiff, waiting for the animal shelter to open up in the morning so I could deliver my legend. They'd tell me it's a shame, she had a good home for awhile, a better life than many animals, but none of that will register. I will be thinking of how she died, how she must've suffered. I will forever be thinking of her eyes. And wondering why I could not learn to read them; wondering if I could foresee the silent, hopeful scream in those that might follow. Right then I has hearing her body slide across the plastic bed liner and bump into the walls of the truck bed.

I've watched enough death in my life. I've seen men fight it all the way to their last gasp, and beyond. Right out of college I worked for a period as a paramedic in a big city, a young man doing a hard job. I was stationed at an inner-city fire station. There were days when I felt like an innocent medic tossed into the jungles of Southeast Asia.

Only we had real docs on the phone and could be at a good hospital in 15 minutes. But when death comes knocking, the sound of its resonating steps, the sound has a kind of universality you might only find when something is born.

"That's it," my young paramedic partner would say after rolling up on an obvious DOA. And we'd call the hospital, get clearance to cease patient care and shut their eyes for them, just like in the movies. But even under the white sheet, I could see tiny muscle twitches, little noises crying out of their mouths.

"Just a natural post-mortem physiological reaction," the doctors had told us in school, "The body's way of cooling down." But I didn't believe it. I was already invested in the legends, way too superstitious or too spiritual to be doing that job. So, after a year or so, I quit. And got myself a dog. Dogs would die of old age while sleeping next to the warm fire and dreaming of when they knew how to catch a Frisbee in mid air only five years ago. I could handle that.

* * *

Three weeks latter, I was better about forgetting, but I'm also quicker to remember. What I'm feeling is that I miss my dog, but I begin to forget the little things, like the way she'd chase her own shadow or stop just before catching a rabbit, as if to say, "Be more careful. I won't eat you but others will."

Forgetting—it's the mind's way of dealing with loss—to dole it out in small palatable bites, like liver to a child. What has sharpened in focus, though, is the reality of what I remember, and now swallow as reconstituted truth: it's that Molly the Brittany spaniel, just another man's dead dog to some, represented what courage and grace could be found in death. She had joined her life and her death, seamlessly, suffering without asking, hurting but giving back, moving out to the edge of the long, dark neighborhood forest and dying alone because she could not heal herself. And those around her, who loved her without even knowing it, who on a normal day would have her with them, had meetings to attend. Life can get in the way of living some times.

Animals are tough like kids are tough. It stems from their innocence. When they hurt they don't look for someone to blame or to sue; they look for comfort and wait for it to pass. Kids grow into adults and are subjected to society's jagged barbs that morph to jingoistic ambivalence. Animals don't read the papers or buy new shoes when they feel bad. They die the way they are born, innocent and wanting to please. And their deaths remind us of how far we have become removed from the purity of youth, begging the question, "What the hell *happened* to me?"

There are good people who die well every day. And there are mean, vicious animals that should be put to sleep. The generalizations are fair and arguable at the same time. But when a good man or a good dog dies, they take with them a part of the living, leaving all that they gave to better the human condition. What Molly took with her was the unconditional love found more often in good dogs than even in good humans. What she left was the hope that it can still exist, that humans still have a chance to catch up.

But sometimes it takes the worst to bring out our best. Like war or tragedy.

They say that many humans lose 21 to 23 grams of weight at the exact moment they die. You couldn't label it evidence of souls, but it can be a comforting thought, when wrestling with your own mortality; the idea that a part of you, maybe the best part or maybe the only part, goes somewhere else. A life-transition is doable. Death seems awfully permanent. And tragedy temporary.

That night as I carried her around looking for a proper resting place, she became heavier, though my memory is that of her feeling lighter the next day. The scales of love and hope could never balance each other; the fluidity and interdependence just too strong for even a momentary equilibrium.

I am haunted by those dying eyes of my dog, cursed to remember so I won't forget. On some early morning runs, my breath coming out like white smoke signals, I have the courage to run alone, to go forth in an attempt to concretize and finally bury what I feel about the way people love, the way they die and the inseparable connection of the two. But as soon as I create the answer, I must erase it; the pain of associated memory coming back up in bites too large to swallow in one meal.

This too, is the way men think of each other in war. After awhile, it's not about nations or battles or even going home. It's about your buddy—staying alive because you'll let him down if you get killed. Any soldier will tell you that. You don't go and get shot because you will disappoint your pals.

I imagine Molly was disappointed that she'd let me down by dying.

And as the sun burns one day into the next, memories of that simple dog-love reshape the past, and then file the edges off the pain and the unvanquished death into a kind of razor's edge of admiration. I think finally, indelibly, that if I *do* know but one thing about dying, it is this: whether you're talking about good or evil, humans or dogs, war or peace, it begins inside, travels to the eyes and ends up in the world.

And there it stays. Living.

In the Name of Our Fathers

"The hero is always the embodiment of man's highest and most powerful aspiration."
Carl Jung

When my son was nine years old, he used to think I could do no wrong. No other father on the block would attempt a fifty/fifty rail slide on a skateboard or drop into a plywood half-pipe. I was his hero and nothing else in this world made me happier. I wear the scars and scabs of skating like a Scoutmaster's badges.

I never doubt these memories. Unlike the clouded sigh of a Disneyland ride, a second grade English teacher or a first love, all of them tainted and twisted by the unbalancing effects of re-interpreted youth, hormones never factor between a father and a son. Male blood lines are immune to nostalgic whim.

Recently, in the footsteps of his older sister, he has come to calling me a "loser" for making him come home before curfew. And when he does I feel like one, even though I know he doesn't mean it. The inner tumult wells up from another place and another time; the feeling will not be denied. Still, in these days of teenage angst, I would give him a kidney same as I'd ask him to mow the lawn.

On those days, I often think back to the time when my own father, just months from dying, would ask me to help out around the house. And I try to convince myself that I did. But I was born with his rebel's heart and it beat defiantly then, as it does now. I would be lying if I said that I'd done all I could for him.

The singer/songwriter, Bob Dylan has said, "To live outside the law, you must be honest." This is the kind of honesty that haunts you all of your days, this striving toward what was and what could've been. To go back and shake that rebel though, and see what truth or consequences fall from his young branches, also may begin to sprout some freedom in the admission.

I began a rough draft of this piece on February 23, 2001. My father would have turned sixty-five that day. He would have been eligible for Social Security and senior discounts at the movies, and no doubt that night we would've toasted his health with a glass of fine cabernet instead of remembering, missing him more than I could write without arcing into high sentiment, my prose taken hostage by the ache of loss. It's an essay that can never be complete, only passed on. Maybe the pain of loss informs our lives more than we can say in words.

He has been dead for over thirty-five years now, since I was a cocky, can-do-no-wrong fifteen-year-old with a restless soul. I have long since passed the age at which he died. But I don't feel old, and I don't think that I will die anytime soon. And I'm no longer afraid of dying the way I once was. I don't think so, anyway.

I suppose that it would be a shame if I weren't able to understand and reconcile his untimely death before I pass as well, to know my hero in death as I knew him in life.

* * *

I would not wish that my father had played a smaller role in my life simply to escape the pain of his dying. I remember when he "procured" an idle ambulance from the sidelines of a football game and took me and my siblings careening through the streets of Orange County, siren blaring, lights flashing. My mother tried to act disgusted. I think of him as an only child, without siblings to fight or to tell scary stories to on a stormy night or to share a tiny bathroom with. He and my mom decided that they were going to have as many as they could make. It was seven and counting when he left us.

I think of him coming home one night from a poker game with the boys, one too many beers involved, and slipping fifty dollars under each child's pillow—in total a big chunk of what he earned in a month. In the morning he told my mom that we deserved it, even though they couldn't afford the luxury, because "kids deserve surprises."

I think of him smiling confidently at the guard at a posh country club as he drove through the gate, flashing an expired Union Oil gas card. "The only ones you should let see your fear," he would tell us, "are the ones who you can trust with it."

He was no saint. He often refused to go to Mass with the rest of the family on Sunday because he'd rather go down to the beach and have his own little bull session with his God. Yes, he had faults, imperfections lost to time and sentimentality and selective memory. He'd gained some weight, lost his patience from time to time. Probably didn't wear a seat belt. But he was a good man. And a lot our own spirit was taken with him. It's hard to break apart a big Catholic family, even if you're a Buddhist.

I find it ironic that I can accept my own eventual death and yet I cannot make sense of his suffering at the hands of a hideous, indiscriminate disease. Urban legend has it that after Neil Armstrong piloted the lunar landing module into the moon's Sea of Tranquility he had trouble parallel parking back on earth. It's supposed to be easier to deal with other people's deaths, easier on earth than in space. I don't know if this angst belongs to the past or the future. But if my house is burning down, I won't agonize over which room to paint first.

The lucky ones defer the question all the way to the end. I don't imagine they die well, knowing that they are dying, but not why.

Perhaps my career choices were guided by a secret desire to cheat death: lifeguard, firefighter, paramedic, professional athlete, and then, at forty, graduate student. And still the grand prize, Enlightenment, eludes me. My dad was my hero. Heroes aren't supposed to die.

Whose fault is that, this death of our heroes? The hero, for being human after all? Ours, for failing to see the inevitable? Who didn't shudder at the sight of actor, Christopher Reeve, strapped to his chair? The mechanical breathing machine that kept him alive out of view, perhaps to shield us from any further reminders of our own fragility—our humanness. Reeve looked disarmingly hopeful, wearing his most courageous public face. Where did his strength come from? The cracked vertebrae came by accident, I know. But was the rest of his life an accident? Let alone his untimely death?

Cartoon heroes are immortal. Everyone knows that.

"There but for the grace of God go I," you think, and change the channel. If Superman can end up a physical prisoner on wheels and then sadly slip away, if my dad can be snatched from his wife and children at the height of his existence, how safe are we in choosing heroes?

Witness the morbid circus that followed the death of stock car racing icon, Dale Earnhardt. Five thousand people attended his televised funeral. For a time after his death, kids in preschool were taught to count by reciting "1-2-Earnhardt-4-5-6-7…" because the number 3 was always Dale's. The guy drove cars at 200 mph for a living, approaching his job no differently than an accountant or an engineer. But he achieved hero status because he did things that most of us can only dream about, shake our heads, nudge our buddies while pointing to the instant replay, "Did you see that?"

Maybe Earnhardt wasn't a hero in the classic sense of folklore: one who commits a selfless act in the service of others. Maybe he was just a very gutsy, talented driver who went over the edge in the regular course of his job. In fact, athlete-heroes may only entertain us with their exploits, impress us with their creative and athletic skill—and yes, their courage—even if it is a diving catch into the grandstands and not a rush into a fiery building. We are tempted to see in athletes elements of heroism that often aren't really there; our hopes and imagination placing us in the netherworld hotel where even they can check in.

But never leave by the same door.

Maybe the men and women who scale the world's great mountains are heroes, not for their incredible feats of physical and mental endurance but for our perception that they have stepped further from earth than the rest of us. It's that mystical barrier, we believe, between this earth and the one beyond. And since no one has yet gone there and returned to describe it, we worship those who can get close enough to touch it, to taste the fruits of the Great Beyond.

What's it like? we ask. The mountain? No. Heaven.

* * *

And what about Reeve? He was simply riding a horse—not an especially dangerous activity. He became a celebrity through a combination of playacting, character type, and mass media exposure. He became a hero to millions through the great irony of this tragedy and his courageous fight to find meaning in what his life had become. All Superman had to do was slip into his spandex tights and red cape to save the world. Reeve had to slip into the interior of his very being to save himself.

I suppose that is part of what I still feel toward my father—the fact that I watched him suffer, watched him stoically endure tremendous physical pain as the cancer slowly and deliberately ate him away. But that was not the worst of it. The worst was that toward the end, he knew that he was going; his trim, surf-tanned body of 170 pounds replaced with a jaundiced shell of 130. He knew he had fought the good fight, done everything possible, made peace with his maker. And all he could do was to wait and try to find some meaning in it. There was nothing else to rebel against.

Some mornings now, as I paddle out before the sun, waiting for its warmth, a few waves before work or class to help make the day more palatable, I too try and find some meaning in it. Yet nearly thirty years and three thousand surf mornings later, I'm not much closer to knowing, except maybe to consider that we aren't supposed to know it at all, which is a kind of meaning.

I can't go back and change what I didn't do, how I didn't spend a few more hours every day with him while he was dying. I can't make the memory of my dad any different. It is a futile wish—a wish to extinguish the last embers of guilt. But making today right can help make yesterday seem less wrong. The beautiful pain of memory is by accident, the painful beauty of imagination by design. At least I know I've tried to be more empathetic with the seriously ill.

* * *

As we grow older, we begin to discover our parents' deficiencies. We notice their quirks and oddities. The hero becomes human, exposing the circularity of the things like water sucked down in a whirlpool as kids sit and wonder where it all goes.

My dad died before I could notice his odd little quirks, before he put on a few pounds around the waist, before his sideburns turned gray, before he might've voted Republican, before hair started to grow in his ears. He died standing atop that pedestal on which a young son places his father, part man, part myth. That's when the stories began to bring him back. Or at least to keep him from going too far.

Two days before he was diagnosed with advanced thoracic cancer, he had complained of back pain from "one too many games of beach volleyball." My mom handed him two aspirin. My older sister called him "soft." He picked up the aspirin and threw them in the pool.

I'd watched him surf that last healthy day, embarrassed; my parents were invading my teenage space. But secretly I wanted to go up to my friends and scream in their ear, "Did you see my dad's last ride? The dude is three times our age and rips!"

As I age, that is the image that grows stronger in my mind, gradually displacing the images of him weak and withered. That is what I want and must hold onto—a single image of a strong, proud young man, regally perched on the tip of his board, arching across large blue waves, white teeth smile, lighthouse visible.

If I hold that one image tight enough and close enough, all the bad ones fade. It is not easy, one moment of his heaven doing battle with eighteen months of our hell. The numbers work against you, but you have your heart on your side. In the end, that has to be enough.

* * *

And just how do heroes come to be? Is it they who follow their hearts, or is it us, the adoring crowd who want to place them in a category that we can strive toward, admire and emulate? Once the hero hears the call to adventure, he will suffer if he denies it more so than he will suffer in the struggle to greatness. We know this from both myth and experience.

But then, as we watch them slip and fall, victims of time, tide and fashion, they still return to us with the knowledge of having lived a hero's existence. Not often do we embrace them for their wisdom. Not often do we glimpse into the darkness from which they have emerged, that place where our metaphysical fear resides.

And then, in that clouded circularity, the hero again becomes victim, disposed of by a disposable society. His foe no longer dragons or evil forces or even age and miles of hard road. It is us, discarding that which we've used.

Their declining beauty and achievement reminds us of our own morality and that the beauty of our youth will soon be replaced with our own truth of loss. Our own mortal decline, hair in the ears and all.

Where we can check out but never leave.

Most of us die too young or too old. At some point we must realize that on some grander scale, life is indeed short and our ego-filled existence utterly insignificant. We try to pull ourselves up by making love, making money, making the grade; all the while making less and less time to face the fact that we can't do it alone. And when we can't, we look to others to do it for us—our heroes. In one way or another, we are all defined in others. This should be celebrated not considered a weakness.

Some time after his career had ended, as his health began to fail, the great Mickey Mantle was spotted by a reporter in a hotel lobby, sitting alone next to a window, listening to the rain bounce off the large, clear panes. When the reporter approached, Mantle held up his hand and said softly to the man, "Listen. It sounds just like applause, doesn't it?"

A hero is born with a warrior's heart, the need to be needed. Sometimes he gets his applause wherever he can.

Maybe the scholar and mythologist, Joseph Campbell, was right when he told us that heroes are chosen in some doctrine of naturalism, some random, before-we-were-born selection process. And we simply go along for the ride either as a participant, an observer, a fan, or an everyman.

This could be said of Christopher Reeve's willingness to go public with his plight, and of Dale Earnhardt accelerating into a turn at 230 mph in hopes of passing one more car. It could be said of Mantle, who played nearly his entire career injured. Every hero pays a price for the privilege, every man a price for his life.

According to Campbell's mythic archetype, the responsibility of heroes is to return to their "tribe" and share the knowledge gleaned on their journey. My dad never recovered from cancer to tell me what it is like to have one's body devoured by metastasizing cells. Yet his struggle was played out for all of us to see—in his jaundiced-eyes and in his immutable will.

And the great Mick, who died from a hereditary disease and complications from alcoholism, was never able to return to the world from which he came and which adored him so. Like most men who give us feats of greatness before they develop feet of clay, his legend is larger than his life.

Carl Jung wrote, "The hero is a hero just because he sees resistance to the forbidden goal in all of life's difficulties and yet fights that resistance with the whole hearted yearning that strives toward the treasure hard to attain, and perhaps unattainable—a yearning that paralyses and kills the ordinary man."

On the baseball diamond, Mickey Mantle was a hero. Off it he was an ordinary man. And it killed him.

I wonder if my dad felt a hero's call. I never had the chance to ask him. On the morning that he died, he called each of us kids into his bed where he lay dying and said goodbye with dignity and prowess, unvanquished to the end. Propped up on three pillows, a little trickle of blood oozing out of the side of his smiling mouth, a hug, a kiss, and a strained voice asking us to take care of each other, as if he were sending us off to summer camp, a sleeping bag in one hand, a note on how to live a good life in the other. And then he was gone.

Tell me. Is there no difference between batting .325 for ten seasons in a row and raising seven kids on $1,000 a month? Does it matter which is greater: to be revered by a few or admired by millions? We need heroes in our lives, although I'm not so sure we know who they are anymore.

Roberto Clemente, arguably the best all-around baseball player of the modern era, is a hero not for his 3,000 hits or his seven Gold Glove Awards. No, I think of

Clemente dying in a plane crash on the way to Nicaragua to help victims of a massive earthquake. For *that,* he was heroic. On the baseball field, he was a very talented athlete. We must not confuse the two.

I wonder if it would have made a difference if my dad had died suddenly and violently, without the eighteen months of gradual and relentless decline. Would he seem more of a hero and less a victim? Would my faith and understanding in his passing be any different if God had simply reached down with His hand and plucked him cleanly from this earth, sparing him the ultimate human embarrassment—bodily impression of a deity's ambivalence?

Sometimes we make our own decisions, sometimes they are made for us. And sometimes the two run together. Some athletes retire at the top of their game so as to never allow the public to witness their inevitable decline. Others, like my dad, have no choice, forced out by injury or illness.

On occasion I try to tell my own son what his grandpa would have been like, how cool it would have been for the three of us to surf together. Most of the time I can't finish the conversation; too much past bubbling up like liquid earth from the core—hot, unstoppable, necessary. One day, when the moment was right, I told my son that my dad would have really liked him, that he might have become a hero to my father. Nine years old, he turned to me and held my shoulders between his little hands, just like I was supposed to hold his, and said, "Yeah but Dad, I bet you were kinda' like his hero too."

Eighteen years on the road, chasing that thin, white fog line up and down the Pacific Coast Highway, chasing chalk lines hastily laid out on the decomposed granite dirt of a high school track, the black tile on the bottom of the pool printed forever on the top of my brain—it was time for me to leave the world of professional athletics.

A little better than average, I may have raced as

though each day was irreplaceable. But for more years than I care to recount, the sun had set on that day and I was losing to kids half my age. I was nobody's athletic hero anymore.

But there was a time, on the front nine of my career, when I impressed enough to earn that cultural label. Once, I was leading a triathlon that had lasted nearly nine hours. With half a mile left to run and two young hotshots breathing down my neck, I had to piss so bad it was killing me. To stop, even to slow down, would cause me to lose the race. Knowing that a precise emotion requires a precise action, I reached down, pulled my shorts to the side, relaxed the appropriate muscles as best I could, and let her fly. The finish line in sight, the crowd cheering, two young speedsters on my heels, urine flying, women pointing, people staring, old men wondering, kids laughing, I thought: fuck 'em all. I crossed the line first and began looking for a cup of water to rinse with.

As I walked away, proud as a damn peacock, an official-looking man approached me and asked, "Mr. Tinley?" I expected he was going to disqualify me and wreck the whole day. He simply stuck his hand out to shake mine, not worried that my fingers were wet with sweat and pee.

"I saw you dig deep," he said. "Really deep. Such survivorship. Almost a vet." Then he walked away, leaving me to wonder at the meaning of his words.

What had I survived? What was I almost a veteran of? A sport? A damn game?

I remembered that day not long ago and wished more than anything that my dad could have been there. Not to see me win, not to see someone call me a hero, but to see me answer a call and follow that path, an exploding rebel soul on a journey of its own and fate's making, regardless of the price. I imagined him seeing himself in me, a reflection made clear with the hand's swipe at a foggy mirror.

If I've learned anything about life, then I must know a little about dying. All I wanted was for my dad to know that I tried. I really tried. And when I think of my son trying, really trying to make me feel better about the death of *my own* dad, I know that he will be a hero to someone, as he already is to me. I will hold his teenage and adult shoulders, look into his eyes as he tries to squirm away, and not worry if mine are full of tears, and I tell him so. If I fail to do that, then God take me now. I am defined by those ahead and behind and all around me. There can be no other way.

Red Tide

Your room looks no different. I stand at the doorway, standing sentinel to the past when Barbie dolls stood in corners awaiting your return; a change of tiny clothes; a ride in the plastic Corvette across the magic carpet of your bedroom floor, wind in their hair from your small, tidy-pursed lips. Their future drove in sync with yours—all wide open.

A light leaks out of the closet and I walk over to turn it off, never remembering when you were old enough to sleep without that luminous lifeguard.

Your room looks the same—unkempt, unruly—like you had just rushed out to meet your friends at the curb, embarrassed for them to see me dressed like them, unkempt, unruly, dangerously close by accident to camo-fatigue and Rasta-colors. I can still smell your perfume, your peppermint incense and your youth. It hurts to breath that deep, to smell that far into the past.

Your room is a place I love, with its Starbucks-colored walls and chambered-waterbed and dry-wilted prom corsages. I love every carpet stain that I scolded you for and remember the Big Red Spot that must've been ink or wine or blood and see the circular replacement of newer carpet as if the groundskeeper has changed the holes on the greens. I laugh, knowing that the ink on this page is me bleeding our loss, your gain, pried open by red grapes and time. I wipe away a tear so as not to leave salt on the past.

Your room still has pictures of you and me. I wonder if your dorm room walls I will grace. I wonder if some college-guy will come in and ask, "That your old man? Can he still surf?" And what will you say to him, this guy, this kid, really, who represents all that lay beyond the horizon while your mother and I watch the sun go down.

In your room, we still exist together. There is tangible evidence: more pictures, wet towels for us to pick up, the lost portable phone, the Eagles CD I've been looking for this past month. In your room the memories are fresh as your child-skin and deep as a knife wound. They are embedded in the sheets you asked me to cuddle you in after a nightmare, entrenched in the blankets that you puked on the first time you stumbled home drunk. Memory's chisel could not re-shape the sweet ghosts that came to us here.

I move across the floor of your room. You've been gone, off to the big city less than a day and your phone rings. I answer and tell the caller that you've gone out, unable to say that you've moved out. Unable to tell the truth, I descend into myself. For I had let a pathetic fallacy slip into my mind—my baby girl would never grow up, would never leave. There is a large white space between then and now. I can't enter into it or reason with myself across it. You've gone away to college, gone away to school. It doesn't matter because you're not here.

The bed in your room is still unmade and I laugh because you are like me—reasoning that a bed will only get messed up each night. Why make it look good for no one else to see? But I see it and pick up your pillow, holding it to my ear like a sea shell a long way from the beach, hoping to hear you call out to me at three in the morning, "Daddy, Daddy, I'm scared. Can you sleep in my bed?" But memory and the rosy-tint of nostalgia are no longer a refuge or a shelter from what must be. Our time with you living with us must be the last true currency of any value. It is sacred, immutable. How selfish of me to want more?

This is how life must change—not one moment or one day at a time but one child-turned adult, one realization that, as Nietzsche said, "Without self-division there is no self-analysis." And so I analyze my angst and watch as it pings and caroms around your room, missing your closet still filled with shoes, your desk piled with things I think you must need but know that you have six of because we bought you four, skipping over the bookshelf with your friends, Seuss and Chopin and Woolf and Porter and Dickenson and DVDs of foreign films that your first boyfriend enjoyed and you sat through with him because it was him. And finally my loss comes back and lands right where it started—in my own pity. It's a place where my nerve endings dance and dangle and finally explode in the realization that all of it was our pleasure, our privilege to raise a child like you.

That summer day when the lightening nearly struck us in Colorado and you refused to leave the house for a week, that time when you crashed your car six days after you had earned your driver's license, that time when your friends couldn't wake you up in the morning and we spent two days in the hospital knowing the OD was, like most adolescent mistakes, not some badge of finality but a right to fuck up, to look in the mirror at eighteen or twenty-eight or fifty-eight and know that you found your center by dancing on your edges. Those are the exacting times that define my years with you as a child, the times that you were my teacher.

I suppose it is the gentle quietness of the room that begins to meld the past with the future, transferring what was with what might be. It stands in contrast to your younger brother's room, still pulsing and beating with the vulnerability of teenage catharsis. I imagine how I might alter the room, maybe dolly it up for guests or turn it into some studio-type cave for the music and art I think will shield me from remembering your seventeen years in this upstairs corner with a view of the neighborhood streets you drew hop-scotch squares on.

But that wears off slowly, like Novocain, and the cloak of self-deceit is replaced by the reality that maybe you'd like to return to your pee-chee folder set, nod politely to your dusty Barbies and chorus of carpet stains;

that you'd rather come home for Thanksgiving or for good and face not a furniture-smashing, gun pulling reunion but slip simply and quietly for a day or a year back into that hallowed brilliance of familiarity. I'd like to think that when you come home and set your suitcase in the middle of the kitchen floor and are pulled like blood to your heart, by the moon's gravity back up to your room, you will lie on the crumpled sheets, smell the sandalwood candles and the fabric softener and see that nothing, really, has changed. Know that then, and forever, as long as you'd like—it is a home.

I can play the wounded vet, a selfish veteran of absence. But not very well.

Screw Thomas Wolfe's notion. Come Thanksgiving we could spill red wine and laugh at the funny shape on the floor. It will go away, as will you, but return, another bottle made better with age; not just time and tide but bound by blood.

Call soon. I won't touch a thing.